TORRENT OF PORTINGALE

Other titles in the Historical Reprint Series:

The Visions of Tundale

Havelok the Dane

Beware the Cat by William Baldwin

King Horn

Sir Gowther and Robert of Sicily

The Unfortunate Traveler by Thomas Nashe

Amoryus and Cleopes by John Metham

Also by Gray Area Press:

Diary of a Heretic by Ross Stein

The Further Travels and Surprising Adventures of Baron Munchausen by Ross Stein

Torrent of Portingale

Torrent of Portingale is a historical work in the public domain

All rights reserved. All original additions, including translations, notes, and glossaries are copyright © 2026 by Gray Area Press and may not be reproduced in any form without written permission from the publisher, except as permitted by U.S. copyright law.

Digital cover image courtesy of The Metropolitan Museum of Art (Creative Commons Zero)

Copyright © 2026 by Gray Area Press

ISBN- 979-8-9934326-1-8

grayareapress.com

Contents

Introduction

The central plot element of *Torrent of Portingale* is as medieval and romantic as one can get. Torrent, the brave but untested son of an earl, falls in love with the beautiful Desonell, daughter of the king of Portugal. To win her for his wife he is tasked by the dubious king to complete a deed of skill and courage: slay a giant who has been menacing the land. Sounds simple, though deadly, enough, and Torrent quickly rises to the challenge.

But *Torrent of Portingale* wouldn't be living up to its label of medieval romance if the story didn't go off the rails right from the start. By the poem's end the titular hero will have slain not one, but five giants, several dragons, ranged as far north as Norway and as far east as the Holy Land, and been betrayed not once, but three times, all to finally win Desonell for his own.

Originally composed in the early 15th century by an unknown author, *Torrent of Portingale* exists today in only one, near complete single manuscript housed in Chetham's Library in Manchester, England. The first modern edition of the poem was published by the English scholar and antiquarian James Halliwell in 1842, with a separate edition by Erich Adam being released in 1887 for the Early English Text Society. Both Halliwell and Adam present the complete poem in its original Middle English format and syntax with additional notes on the text.

Middle English is not your grandfather's English. It's not your great-grandfather's either. Evolving out of the Old English period (700s-1066), and heavily influenced by Old Norse, Old French, and Old Norman, the Middle English period saw major grammatical changes including, but not limited to, inflection, verb conjugation, pronoun usage, and word order. The alphabet was not immune to these changes either. Over the course of several centuries, Latin holdover characters from Old English like yogh† [ȝ], wynn [ƿ], and thorn [þ] fell out of usage, replaced by the more familiar [gh], [w], and [th] we use in contemporary English today.

This Gray Area Press Historical Reprint Series edition seeks to lessen the challenges today's reader will encounter interpreting Middle English by presenting *Torrent of Portingale* in two distinct side-by-side versions. The first is an exact reprint of Adam's 1887 edited version[‡] with no changes, while the second version has been updated using contemporary English conventions and attempts to retain the story's poetic structure while simultaneously providing a translation of alphabet and vocabulary from Middle to contemporary modern English. Mayhew and Skeats' *A Concise Dictionary of Middle English From A.D. 1150 To 1580* (1888) proved an invaluable resource in this endeavor, as did the University of Michigan's online Middle English Compendium. But attempt is an operative word, as this approach too is not without its sacrifices, and the reader will note multiple instances throughout the text where the rhyme scheme is distorted (or in many instances completely destroyed) by these translations. Nevertheless, rhyme scheme and other grammatical conventions, including some punctuation conventions, were purposefully ignored in favor of presenting the story of Torrent of Portingale in as close to the original Middle English form as possible. Attempts to preserve consistent verb tense and the select application of adverbs for clarity was also implemented throughout the text to facilitate ease of meaning.

Finally, periodic explanatory notes have been placed throughout the text to aid the reader in following the story.

† Note the ME character yogh [ȝ] is often indistinguishable from the ME character [z] which often included a curved tail. This text includes multiple instances of the word Naȝareth which should be read and pronounced accordingly.

‡ "Torrent of Portyngale. Re-edited from the unique ms. in the Chetham Library, Manchester, by E. Adam, PH. D." In the digital collection Corpus of Middle English Prose and Verse. https://name.umdl.umich.edu/CME00056. University of Michigan Library Digital Collections.

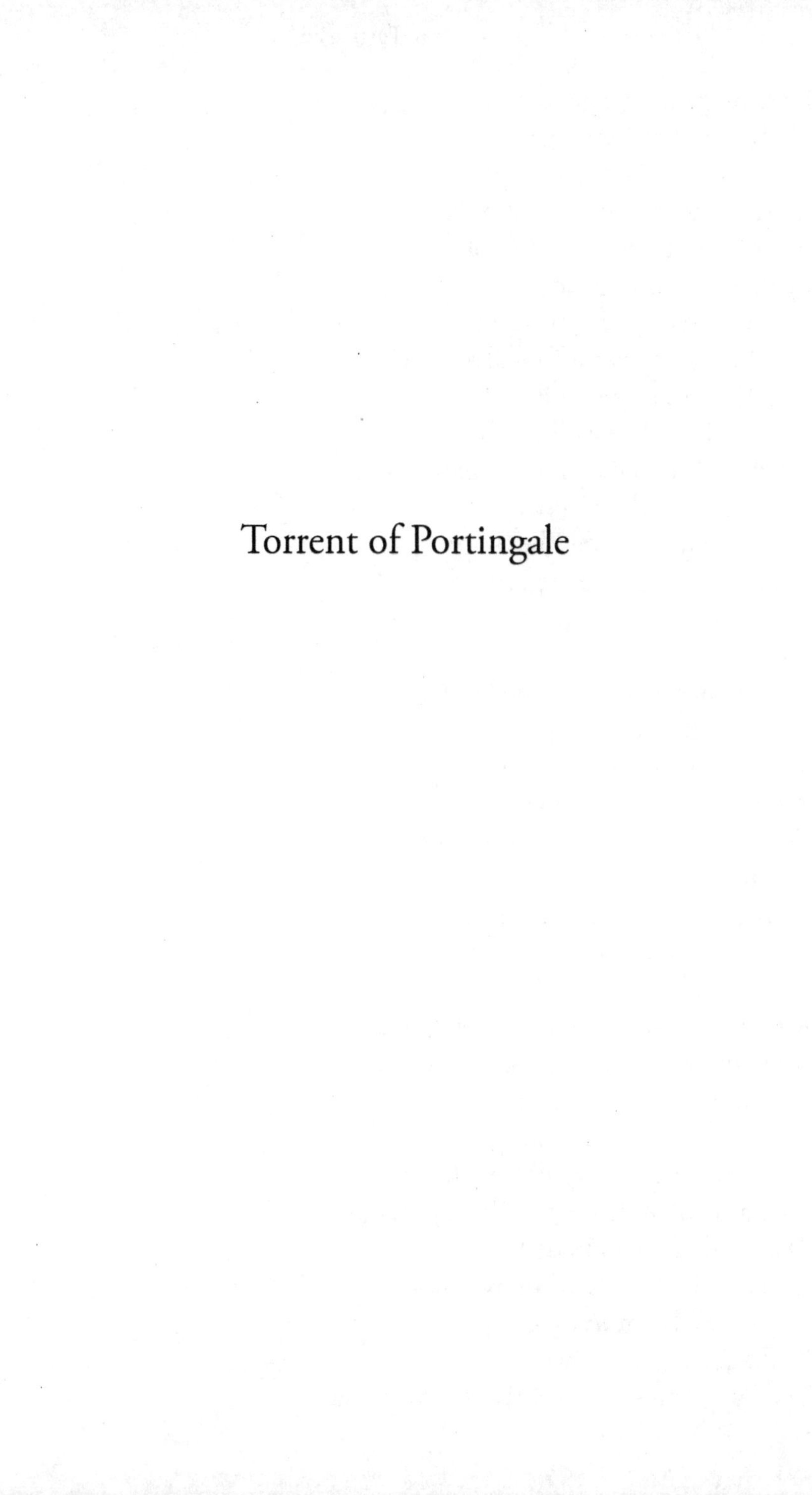

Torrent of Portingale

Here bygynneth a good tale
Of Torrente of Portyngale.

GOD, that ys worthy and Bold,
Heuen and Erthe haue In hold,
Fyld, watyr, and wynde,
Yeve vse grace hevyn to wyne,
And brynge vs owt off Dedly synne
And In thy seruyse to Ende!
A stounde and ye wołł lyst be-Dene,
Ale dowghtty men þat Euyr hathe ben,
Wher So that they lende,
I Schałł yow tełł, ore I hense pase,
Off a knyght, þat Dowghtty wase,
In Rome ase clarkys ffynde.

In Portynggałł, that Ryche londe,
An Erełł that wase wonande,
That curtese wase and wyght;
Sone aftyr he had a sone,
The feyerest þat on fot myght gon,
Tyrrant, men seyd, he hyght.
Be tyme he wase XVIII yer old,
Of deddes of armys he wase bold,
To felle bothe kyng and knyght;
And now commythe dethe appon a day
And takythe hys father, ase I yow sey,
For God ys most of myght.

The kyng of Portynggałł wase fayne,
To-warde hym he takythe Torrayne,
That Dowghtty ys in dedde;
And ther he fesomnyd in hys hond
A good Eyrldom in that lond,
Bothe forest and downe.
The kyng hathe a dowghttyr whyte ase fame,

Here begins a good tale
Of Torrent of Portugal.

God, that is worthy and bold,
Who has heaven and earth in hand,
Field, water, and wind,
Gives us grace to win heaven,
And brings us out of deadly sin
And in your service to the end!
Wait a time and you will hear entirely,
All brave men that ever have been,
Where so that they land,
I shall tell you, before I pass hence,
Of a knight, that was brave,
In Rome as clerics find.

> The narrator begins the tale of a brave young man named Torrent, the son of an earl in the land of Portugal. Though not himself a knight, Torrent is strong in battle and can best most knights in combat.
>
> Torrent is favored by the king of Portugal and grants him his own earldom. But Torrent has eyes for Desonell, the beautiful daughter of the king.

In Portugal, that rich land,
An earl was living,
That was courteous and valiant.
Soon after he had a son,
The fairest that might have gone on foot,
Torrent, men said, he was called.
By the time he was eighteen years old,
Of deeds of arms he was bold,
To fell both king and knight.
And now came death upon a day
And took his father, as I say to you,
For God is of most might.

The king of Portugal was happy.
Toward him he took Torrent,
That was brave in deed.
And there he gave in his hand
A good earldom in that land,
Both forest and down.
The king had a daughter white in fame,

Dysonell wase her name,
Worthyest in wede.
When Torrent had of her a syght,
More he lovyd that swete wyght
Than ałł ys fathyrys lede.

For love of thys lady Deyr
In dede of armys far and nere
Aventorres gan he take
With heve tymbyr and ovyr-Ryde,
Ther myght no man hys dent a-bydde,
But to the Erthe he them strake.
Her father and other knyghttes mo
Had farly, how he Ryd soo,
And on a day to hyme spake,
He Seyd: ' Torrent, howe may thys byne,
That thow Dyspisyst thes knyghttes kene
And ordurres non wołł take?'

Torrent sayd: 'So mvt I the,
An other sayment wołł I see,
Ore I take ordor of knyght.'
Tho he sware be hevyn kyng,
Ther wase told hym a wondyr-thyng
In hys chambyr to nyght:
'For the love of my doughter dere
Thow makyst good far and nere
In Dedde of armys bryght;
And wyt thow wyłł, so god me saue,
Thow schalt her wyne, yf thow her haue,
Be thow neuyr so wyght!'

Torrent sayd: 'Be Marry dere,
And I were off armyse clere,
Yowr Dowghttyr me leve were.'
The kyng seyd: 'Yf yt be soo,

Desonell was her name,
In noble garments.
When Torrent had sight of her,
More he loved that sweet creature
Than all his father's land.

For love of this lady dear
In deed of arms far and near
Adventures he took
With heavy lance and over ground,
There might no man abide his strikes,
But to the earth he struck them.
Her father and other knights too
Marveled, how he rode so,
And one day spoke to him.
He said, "How may this be,
That you displease these bold knights
And will take no orders?"

To impress Desonell, Torrent takes on many adventures, risking his life and besting other knights to demonstrate his worth and prowess. Despite all of this, Torrent refuses to take the orders of a knight until he can accomplish a great test of might.

Torrent said, "So must I,
Another test will I see,
Before I take the orders of the knight."
Then he swore by heaven's king,
A wonderful thing was told to him
In his chamber that night,
"For the love of my daughter dear
You make good far and near
In deed of arms bright;
And I know your will, so God save me,
You shall win her, if you will have her,
Be you never so brave!"

The king of Portugal approaches Torrent to undertake a feat of bravery alone. He tells Torrent Desonell will be his if he accomplishes this feat.

Torrent said, "By Mary dear,
If I were of arms glorious,
Your daughter would love me."
The king said, "If it be so,

Ore VII yere be a-go,
More schałł we here:
Durst thow, for my dowghttyr sake,
A poynt of armys for to take
With-owt helpe of fere?'
Than seyd Torrant: 'So god me sped,
With anny man that syttythe on stede
Other far ore nere!'

Ther-of the kyng for tene wax wode:
'Yf thow wylt make thy body good,
Be trew and hold thy contenance . . . .
Tho seyd Torrant: 'So god me sped ere!
And I wyst, in what sted they were,
Fore no man wold I chaunce.'

'In to the Grekes see a mylle
Ther lyvythe a gyant in an yle,
Fułł Euyłł thow dourst hyme stond.
My fayer forestes fellythe downe he
And Ryche castelles in that contre,
No ston lettythe he stond.'

Terrent sayd: 'Be Marre bryght,
Yt ys gret sorrow that he hathe syght,
The devyłł of hełł hym blynd!'
The kyng sayd: 'Par la-more de dewe,
Thow darryst fułł evyłł with thy Ey hym sewe,
He wold fełł the with hys wynde.'
'Now, be my trowthe,' seyd Torrent than,
'Ase I ame a jentylman,
Yf I may hym fynd,
Won fot wołł I not fro hym pase,
Thow he be stronger than Samson wase,
Or anny man of hys kynd!'

Before seven years be gone,
More shall we hear.
Dare you, for my daughter's sake,
A feat of arms to take
Without help of companions?"
Then Torrent said, "So God help me,
With any man that sits on steed
Either far or near!"

Thereof the king grew vexed from madness,
"If you will make your body good,
Be true and hold your conduct . . . .
Then Torrent said, "So God help me before!
And I knew, in what place they were,
For no man would I not hazard."

The king, secretly vexed by Torrent's love for his daughter, tells him of a giant living on an island wreaking havoc on the land and castles. Torrent must slay this giant by himself.

"Into the Greek sea a mile
There lives a giant on an island,
Fully evil there does he stand.
He felled my fair forests
And rich castles in that country,
He let none stand."

Torrent said, "By Mary bright,
It is great sorrow that he has sight,
The devil of hell blind him!"
The king said, "For the love of God,
Though you dare, if with his evil eye he saw you,
He would fell you with his wind."
"Now, by my truth," Torrent said then,
"As I am a gentleman,
If I may find him,
One foot will I not pass from him,
Though he be stronger than Samson was,
Or any man of his kind!"

Hys squyerys, they mornyd sare,
With-owt fere that he schold fare
To that gret iorney,
With the gyant heygh for to fyght.
Be-gon-mese that gyant hyght,
That fynddes fere for aye.
To arme hyme Torrant gas,
Hys good stede with hym he tas,
With owt squyer that Day.
He takythe leve at lorddys hend,
And on hys wey gan he wynd,
For hym ałł they pray.

Lytyłł wyst Desonełł that jente,
For whos love that he went
To fyght with that knave.
Now god, that Dyed appon a Rode,
Strengithe hym bothe bone and blod,
The fyld for to haue!
He that schałł wend soche a wey,
Yt were nede for hym to pray,
That Iesu hym schuld saue.
Yt ys in the boke of Rome,
Ther was no knyght of kyrstendome,
That jorney Durst crave.

VI days Rydythe he
By the cost of the feyer see,
To seke the gyant kene.
By the cost as he Rode,
In a forest longe and brode
And symly wase to sene,
Hey sperrys ther he fonde
And gret olyvys growonde
Coverd in levys grene.
Sone wase he ware, ase y yow say,

His squires, they mourned sorely,
That without companions he should fare
On that great journey,
To fight with the giant high.
Begonmese that giant was called,
That fiend's company forever.
Torrent went to arm himself,
His good steed with him he took,
Without squire that day.
He took leave at his lord's hand,
And on his way he went,
For him they all prayed.

Torrent resolves to fight the giant alone as the king asks to win the hand of Desonell. For her part, Desonell is unaware that Torrent has feelings for her and does not know the true reason he sets off to fight the giant.

Little knew Desonell, that gentlewoman,
For whose love that he went
To fight with that knave.
Now God, that died upon a cross,
Strengthened him in both bone and blood,
To have the field!
He that shall go such a way
It was needed for him to pray,
That Jesus should save him.
It is in the book of Rome,
There was no knight in Christendom,
That dared crave that journey.

Six days he rode
By the coast of the fair sea,
To seek the bold giant.
By the coast as he rode,
In a forest long and broad
And was seemly to see,
High grass he found there
And great olives growing
Covered in green leaves.
Soon he was aware, as I tell you,

Vppon a movnteyn ther he laye
On slepe, ase I wene.

Torrent, on kne knelyd he
And be-sowght Jesu so fre,
That bowght hym with hys blod:
'Lord, ase thow dyd ryght for Mary,
Let me never take velony
And gef me of thy fode!
Serttes, yf I hym slepyng slone,
Manfułł Ded were yt none
For my body, be the Rode.'
Tho Terrant blewe hys bugełł bold,
To loke that he a-wake wold,
And sythe ner hyme Rode.

So fast a-slepe he wase browght,
Hys hornys blast a-woke hyme nowght,
He swellyd ase dothe the see.
Torrent saw, he wołł not wake,
He Reynyd hys sted vnto a stake,
Ase a jentyłł man so fre.
So hy, he say, wase the movnteyne,
Ther myght no horse wynd hym a-geyn
But yf he nowyd wold be;
Thowe the wey neuyr so wykkyd ware,
On hys wey gan he fare,
In gret perayłł went hee.

Torent went to that movnteyn,
He put hys spere hyme a-geyne,
'A-Ryse, fellow!' gan he saye;
'Who made the so bold here to dwełł,
My lordes frethe thus to fełł?
A-mendes the be-hovythe to pay.'
The gyant Rysythe, ase he had byn wod,

Upon a mountain where he lay
Asleep, as I know.

After a six-day ride Torrent finds the giant sleeping atop a mountain. Believing that killing his enemy while he sleeps would be dishonorable, Torrent rides close to the giant and sounds his battle horn to wake him.

Torrent knelt on his knee
And besought Jesus so free,
That bought him with his blood.
"Lord, as you did right for Mary
Let me never take wickedness
And give me of your food!
Certainly, if I slay him sleeping,
It would not be a brave deed
For my body, by the cross."
Then Torrent boldly blew his bugle
To ensure that he would awake,
And after rode near him.

So fast asleep he was brought
His horn blast woke him not,
He swelled as does the sea.
Torrent saw, he would not wake,
He tied his steed to a stake,
As a gentleman so free.
So high, he saw, was the mountain,
No horse might carry him there
Unless he were mad;
Though the way was never so wicked,
On his way he did fare,
In great peril he went.

Torrent's horn blast fails to wake the giant, so he approaches his enemy and prods him awake with his spear.

Torrent went to that mountain,
He put his spear against him,
"Arise, fellow!" he said,
"Who made you so bold to dwell here,
And fell my lord's forest?
It behooves you to pay amends."
The giant rose, as if he were mad,

And Redyly by hyme stode,
Be-syd hyme on a lay,
And seyd: 'Sertes, yf I leve,
Soche a wed I wołł the geff,
To meve the Euyr and ay.'

Thow the chyld were neuyr so yinge,
The fyndes spere sparrythe hyme no-thyng
In the holttes haree;
Who had fare and nere byne,
And neuer had of fytyng syn,
He myght a lernyd thare.
The gyant, the fyrst stroke to hym he cast,
His good schyld ałł to-brast,
In schevyres spred wase yare;
Tho covd he no bettur Red,
But stond styłł, tyłł one were ded;
The gyant lefte hym thar.

Torrent vndyr hys spryt he sprent
And a-bowght the body he hyme hente,
As far as he myght last.
'A! fellow, wylt thow so?'
And to the grownd gan they goo,
Of the movnteyn bothe downe they past.
Ase the boke of Rome tellys,
They tornyd XXXII ellys,
In armys walloyng fast.
Yt tellythe in the boke of Rome,
Euyr ase the gyant a-boue come,
Hys guttes owt of hys body brast.

At the fot of the movnteyn
Ther lay a gret Ragyd ston, serteyn,
Yt nyhed ys schuldyr bon
And also hys Ryght syd,

And readily stood by him,
Beside him on a lake,
And said, "Certainly, if I leave,
Such a payment I would give you,
To move you ever and all."

Torrent and the giant exchange threats before engaging in combat. The giant fiercely attacks Torrent, shattering his shield.

Though the child were never so young,
The fiend's spear spared him nothing
In the filthy woods;
Who had far and near been,
And never had of fighting sin,
He might have learned there.
The giant, the first stroke to him he cast,
Burst his good shield,
Completely to splinters;
Though could he no better think,
But stood still, as one who were dead;
The giant left him there.

Torrent under his spear sprinted
And about the body he seized,
As far as he might last.
"Ah! fellow, will you so?"
And to the ground they did go,
Off the mountain both down they passed.
As the book of Rome tells,
They turned thirty-two times,
In arms tumbling fast.
It tells in the book of Rome,
As the giant came from above,
His guts burst out of his body.

Torrent plays dead to catch the giant unawares. He leaps on his enemy and the two tumble off the mountaintop where the giant's body is torn open by the impact.

At the foot of the mountain
There lay a great ragged stone, certainly,
It injured his shoulder bone
And also his right side,

Ther to that gyant fełł that tyd,
Ase I herd in Rome . . . .

Thorrow hyme, that mad man,
Torrent sone a-bovyn wane
And fast he gan him quelle
With a knyffe feyer and bryght;
Torrent, with ałł hys myght
Ther-with he gard hyme dwełł.

Torent knelyd on hys kne,
To Iesu Cryst prayd he,
That hathe thys world to wyld:
'Lord, lovyd, evyr lovyd thowe be,
The feyer fyld thow hast lent Me,'
—Vpp bothe hys handes he held—
'Ałł onely with-owt any knaue
Of the fynd the maystry to haue,
Of hym to wyn the fyld.'
Now ys ther none other to say,
Of hyme he wane the fyld þat day;
I pray God hyme schyld.

Torrent went vppe a-geyne
To the movnt, ase I gan sayne,
The londes to se far and nere;
In the see a myle, hyme thoȝt,
An hold wase Rychyly wrowt,
In that lond wase not here perre.
The see wase Ebbyd, I yow sey,
Torrent thether toke the way,
Werry ałł thow he were;
And ther he fownd Ryche wonys,
Towrres Endentyd with presyos stonys,
Schynyng ase crystałł clere.

There to that giant fell that time
As I heard in Rome . . .

Torrent quickly beheads the gravely injured giant.

Through him, that mad man,
Torrent soon went above
And quick he did kill him
With a knife fair and bright;
Torrent, with all his might
Therewith took care of him.

Torrent knelt on his knee,
To Jesus Christ he prayed,
That has this world to wield.
"Lord, loved, ever loved you be,
The fairer field you have lent me,"
—He held up both hands—
"Alone, without any servant
Of the fiend to have the mastery,
Of him to win the field."
Now is there nothing other to say,
Of him he won the field that day;
I pray God shield him.

Torrent climbs back up the mountain and spies a castle in the distance. He rides there and finds the place richly adorned.

Torrent went up again
To the mountain, as I said,
To see the lands far and near;
In the sea a mile, he thought,
A hold was richly wrought,
In that land was not her peer.
The sea was ebbed, I tell you,
Torrent thither took the way,
Although he was weary;
And there he found a rich dwelling,
Towers encrusted with precious stones,
Shining as clear crystal.

Two gattys off yron ther he fond,
Ther in Torrent gan wonde,
A nyghtes Rest there in to ta;
And at the hale dore ther wase
A lyon & a lyonasse,
Ther men be-twene them twa
Fast Etyng, ase ye may here;
Crystyn man thow he were,
Hys browys wexe bla,
And wit yow wiłł, lord god yt wote,
He durst goo no fote,
Lest they wold hyme sla.

Torrant stod and be-held,
And prayd to god, that ale may wyld,
To send hyme harborrow good.
Sone hard he within a whalle
The syghyng of a lady smalle,
Sche weppte, as sche were wod;
Sche mornyd sore and sayd: 'Alas,
That Euyr kynges dowghttyr wase
Ouer-come of so jentyłł blod,
For now ame I holdyn⊠ here
In lond with a fyndes fere!'
Torrent hard, wher he stod.

Dere god,' seyd Torrant than,
'Yff ther be anny crystyn man
In thys hold of ston,
That wołł, for the love of god of myght,
Harbourrow a jentylman thys nyght,
For I ame but on!'
'Seynt Marry,' seyd that lady clere,
'What crystyn man axithe harburrow here?'
Nere hym sche gothe a-non.
'I wold harburrow the fułł fayne,

Two gates of iron there he found,
Therein Torrent went,
A night's rest therein he wished to take;
And at the hall door there was
A lion and a lioness,
Two men between them
Eating quickly, as you may hear;
Though a Christian man he was,
His brows grew pale,
And know you will, lord God knows it,
He dared go no further,
Lest they would slay him.

Torrent seeks to rest in the castle after his battle with the giant, but he finds two lions guarding the entrance.

Torrent stood and beheld,
And prayed to God, that may wield all,
To send him good harbor.
Soon he heard within the walls
The sighing of a lady small,
She wept, as if she were mad;
She mourned sorely and said, "Alas,
That ever king's daughter was
Overcome of so noble blood,
For now am I held here
In a land with a fiend's company!"
Torrent heard, where he stood.

Torrent hears the sound of a woman weeping coming from within the castle. He calls out and a lady answers. He asks for shelter, but she warns him to leave, lest the giant return and kill him.

"Dear God," Torrent said then,
"If there be any Christian man
In this hold of stone,
That will, for the love of God of might,
Harbor a gentleman this night,
For I am but one!"
"Saint Mary," said that lady clear,
"What Christian man asks harbor here?"
She went near him at once.
"I would harbor you full willingly,

But a gyant wyłł the slayne.'
To hym sche mad here mone.

'Say me now, fayer lady, belyve,
Who owte of thys plase schałł me dryve,
Thes tourres, that are so bryght?'
Ther sche Seyd: 'Be hevyn kyng,
Here ys a gyant Dwellyng,
That meche ys of myght.
Be my trowthe, and he the see,
Were ther XX lyvys in the,
Thy dethe than wyłł he dyght.
Iesu cryst yef me grace
To hyd the in some preve plase
Owt of the fyndes syght! . . . .

'Euyr me thynkythe be thy tale,
The song of the burdes smale
On slepe hathe hyme browght.'
'Ye,' seyd Torrent, 'ore he be wakyn,
I schałł the tełł soche a tokyn,
Of hym thow haue no thowght!
But wolddes thow for thy gentry
Do the lyonnys downe lye,
That they nyee me nowght?'
By the hande sche ganne hym ta
And led hyme in betwe them twa;
Ryght ase sche wold, they wrowght.

The lady wase neuyr so a-drad,
In to the hale sche hym lad,
That lemyred ase gold bryght;
Sche byrlyd whyt wyne and Rede:
'Make vse myrre a-geyne owre Dedd,
I wot wiłł, yt ys so dyght!'
'Be my trowthe!' seyd Torrent,

But a giant will kill you."
She made her moan to him.

"Tell me now, fair lady, believe,
Who shall drive me out of
These towers that are so bright?"
There she said, "By heaven's king,
Here a giant is living,
That is of much might.
By my truth, if he sees you,
Were there twenty lives in you,
Your death then will he prepare.
Jesus Christ give me grace
To hide in some private place
Out of the fiend's sight!" . . . .

"Ever I think by your tale,
The song of the small birds
That sleep has brought him."
"Yes," said Torrent, "before he wakes,
I shall tell you such a token,
Of him though have no thought!
But would for your gentry
Do the lions lie down,
That they come not near me?"
By the hand she took him
And led him in between the twain;
Right as she would, they behaved.

The lady comes out to meet Torrent and invite him inside thinking they will both be killed when the giant returns. Torrent is surprised when the lions heel in her presence and don't attack either of them.

Inside the castle, the lady feeds Torrent and tells him they will surely die. Torrent tells her to worry no longer, as the giant was recently killed by a young knight.

The lady was never so adread,
Into the hall she led him,
That shined as bright gold;
She offered white wine and red.
"Make us merry again before our death,
I know it will, it is so prepared!"
"By my truth!" Torrent said,

'I wole be thy warrant,
He comythe not here thys nyght.
On soche a slepe he ys browght,
Ałł men of lyve wakythe hym nowght,
But onely godes myght.'

Blythe then wase that lady jent,
For to on-harnes Torrent,
That dowghtty wase and bold;
'For sothe,' sche seyd, 'I wot wher ys
The kynges sone Verdownys,
Fast put in hold
In a dongon, that ys dym;
Fowyre good Erylles sonnys be with hyme
Ys fet in fere and fold.
The gyant wan theme in a tyde,
Ase they Rane be the watyr syd,
And put them in preson cold.

'In an yron cage he hathe them done.'
Torrent went thether sone:
'Are ye yet levand?'
The kynges sone askyd than,
Yf ther were anny crysten man,
'Wold bryng vse owt of bond?'
'Lord,' he seyd, 'god ałłmyght,
I had levyr on a Day to fyght,
Than ałł my fathyrys lond.'
With an iryn małł styff and strong
He brake vpe an yron dore or longe,
And sone the keyes he fond.

Owt he toke thys chyldyryn fyve,
The feyrest that were on lyve,
I-hold in anny sted.
The lady wase fułł gled,

"I will be your guard,
He comes not here this night.
On such a sleep he is brought,
All men alive wake him not,
But only God's might."

Thrilled to learn the giant is dead, the lady tells Torrent there are five additional prisoners in the castle dungeon, one of whom is the son of the king of Verdon.

Torrent quickly rushes to the dungeon and frees the prisoners.

Joyful then was that gentle lady,
To unharness Torrent,
That was brave and bold;
"For truth," she said, "I know where is
The king of Verdon's son.
Put in a hold
In a dungeon, that is dim;
Four good earls' sons are with him
Fettered in company and fold.
The giant won them in a time,
As they ran by the waterside,
And put them in the cold prison.

"In an iron cage he has them."
Torrent went thither soon,
"Are you yet living?"
The king's son asked then,
If there were any Christian men,
"Would bring us out of bondage?"
"Lord," he said, "God almighty,
I had rather on a day to fight,
Than all my father's land."
With an iron mail stiff and strong
He broke up the iron door before long,
And soon the keys he found.

Out he took these children five,
The fairest that were alive,
I believe in any stead.
The lady was fully glad,

Sche byrlyd whyt wyn and Redd,
And sethyn to soper sone they yed.
'Lordes,' he seyd, 'syn yow are her,
I Red yow make Ryght good cher,
For now ys ał thy nede.'
Thus he covyrd owt of care.
God, that sofryd wonddes sare,
Grante vse weł to sped!

Lorddes, and ye wol lythe,
The chyldyr namys I woł teł blythe,
Here kyn, how they were me told;
The kynges sone, that dowghtty ys,
Wase clepyd Verdownys,
That dowghtty wase and bold,
And an Erylles son, that hyght Torren,
A nother Iakys of Berweyne,
The forthe was Amyas bold.
The kynges dowghttyr of Gales lond,
Elyoner, I vndyrstond,
That worthy wase in hold,

In to hys chambyr sche hyme led,
Ther gold and syluyr wase spred,
And asur, that wase blo;
In yron ther he gan stond,
Body and armys al schynand,
In powynt to trusse and goo.
In to a stabył sche hym led,
Eche toke a fuł feyer sted,
They were redy to goo;
And wote ye weł and vndyrstond,
Had the gyant be levand,
They had not partyd soo.

They woł not to bed gange,

She poured white wine and red,
And after to supper soon they went.
"Lords," he said, "since you are here,
I advise you make right good cheer,
For now is all your need."
Thus they recovered out of grief.
God, that suffered wounds sore,
Grant us well good fortune!

Lords, if you will listen,
The children's names I will happily tell,
Hearken, how they were told to me;
The king's son, who is brave,
Was called Verdon,
Who brave was and bold,
And an earl's son, called Torren,
Another Jakys of Berwen,
The fourth was Amyas bold.
The king's daughter of Galicia,
Eleanor, I understand,
Was worthy and gracious,

> We learn the names of the five noble prisoners and that the lady is Eleanor, a princess of Galicia.
>
> Eleanor leads Torrent to a treasure room in the castle.

Into his chamber she led him,
There gold and silver was spread,
And azure, that was blue;
In iron there he stood,
Body and armor all shining,
Arranged to pack and go.
Into a stable she led him,
Each took a full fair steed,
They were ready to go;
And know you well and understand,
Had the giant been living,
They had not parted so.

They would not go to bed,

Tyłł on the morrow the Day spronge,
Thus a wey to ffare.

Torrant sperryd the gattys, i-wyse,
Ałł that he lyst he clepyd hys,
The keys and thyng he bare.
The lyons that was at the dore
Wase led to her mayster that wase befor,
On hym thay fed them yare,
Vpp won of the horse, that wase ther levyd,
On hym thei trussyd the gyanttes heved.
Thus helpt hym god thar.

But ore III wekes wer commyn to End,
To Portynggałł gan he wend,
Ther ase the kyng gan lend;
The porter sawe hym ther he stood,
He fled a wey, ase he were wod,
Flyngyng ase a fynd.
'Syr kyng,' he seyd, 'be goddes dede,
Torrant bryngythe a devyłł ys hed,
Ther with he wołł yow present.'
Desonełł seyd: 'Porter, be styłł!' . . . .
In hys walke ther ase he went.

The kyng to the gatys gan pase,
Gret lordes that ther wase,
Bothe knyghtes and squyerre,
Lordes wase fułł sore a-dred
Fore the lyonys, þat he had,
They durst not come hyme ner.
The kyng seyd: 'I wyłł the kysse,
Durst I for thy bestes, Iwysse.'
Torrent dyd them ly ther,
And kyssyd the kyng with joy and blyse;
And aftyr, other lordes of hys,

Till on the morrow the day sprung,
Thus a way to fare.

Torrent fastened the gates, I know,
All that he liked he called his,
The keys and things he bore.
The lions that were at the door,
Were led to their master that was before,
On him they fed,
Upon one of the horses, that lived here,
On him they trussed the giant's head.
Thus God helped him there.

Taking horses from the giant's stable, Torrent, Eleanor. and the others ride out. Torrent takes the lions to the giant's corpse and they devour it. He hangs the giant's severed head as a trophy from his saddle and takes the lions, now tamed, with him.

But before three weeks came to an end,
To Portugal he went,
There as the king lived;
The porter saw him standing there,
He fled away, as if he were mad,
Flailing as a fiend.
"Sir king," he said, "by God's deed,
Torrent brings a devil's head,
Therewith he will present it to you."
Desonell said, "Porter, be still!" . . . .
In his walk there as he went.

Torrent and company return to Portugal with his trophy and the lions. He is greeted by the king and other nobles, who are afeared by the sight of the beasts.

The king went past the gates,
Great lords were there,
Both knights and squires.
The lords were full of dread,
For the lions that he had.
They dared not come near him.
The king said, "I would kiss you,
If not for your beasts."
Torrent made them lie there,
And kissed the king with joy and bliss;
And after, other lords of his,

And aftyr, ladys clere.

Messengyres went the weye,
To the kyng of Provyns to sey,
Hys sone ys owt of hold:
'Yyng Torrent of Portynggałł
Hathe browght hym owt of balle
And slayne the jeyant bold.'
Lytyłł and mykyłł þat ther wer,
Ałł they mad good cher
Her prynse fayne se wold.
The kyng seyd: 'So mot I the,
I wołł geff the towynnys thre
For the talles thow hast me told.'

Than seyd they, that to Gales yede,
Yeftys to take were hem no ned,
Then Verdownys had they.
Ase they seylyd on a tyde,
At Perrown on the see syd
. . . .
The kyng of Provynse seyd: 'So mot I the,
Yftles schałł they not be,
That dare I sothely sey.'
The kyng of Gales proferd hym feyer:
'Wed my dowghttyr and myn Eyer,
When so euyr thow may! . . . .

The kyng of Pervense seyd: 'So mot I the,
Thys seson yeftles schałł thow not be,
Iaue here my Ryng of gold,
My sword, that so wyłł ys wrowyt;
A better than yt know I nowght
With in crystyn mold;
Yt ys ase glemyrryng ase the glase,
Thorrow Velond wroght yt wase,

And after, ladies fair.

Messengers went the way,
To the king of Provence[1] to say,
His son is out of bondage.
"Young Torrent of Portugal
Has brought him out of misfortune,
And slain the bold giant."
Little and many that there were,
They all made good cheer
To gladly see their prince.
The king said, "So must I,
I will give you three towns
For the tales you have told me."

Messengers are sent to the king of Provence to tell him his son, the prince of Verdon, was rescued.

Then they said, that to Galicia went,
Gifts to take to him were not wanting,
Then Verdon they had.
As they sailed on a tide,
At Perrown[2] on the seaside
. . . .
The king of Provence said, "So may I,
Gift less shall they not be,
That dare I truthfully say."
The king of Galicia proffered him fair,
"Wed my daughter and my heir,
When so ever you may! . . . .

A missing section of the manuscript. It can be inferred that Torrent visits Galicia to return the princess and receive further gifts. before going back to Provence.

The king of Galicia offers his daughter Eleanor in marriage, which Torrent refuses.

The king of Provence said, "So must I,
This season gift less you shall not be.
Have here my ring of gold,
My sword, that so well is wrought;
A better one than it I know not
Within Christendom made;
It is as glimmering as glass,
It was made by Wayland[3],

The king of Provence gives Torrent his sword, called Adolake, which was made by Wayland.

Bettyr ys non to hold.
I have syne sum tyme in lond,
Whoso had yt of myn hond,
Fawe they were I-told.'

Tho wase Torrent blythe and glad,
The good swerd ther he had,
The name wase Adolake.
A gret maynerey let he make ryght
That lest ałł a fortnyght,
Who so wiłł hys met take.
Euyry man toke ys leve, ase I yow say,
Hom-ward to wend ther wey,
Euery man ys Rest to take.
Tyłł yt be-fełł vppon a day,
Ase they went be the wey,
The kyng to hys dowghttyr spake:

'Ye schałł take hed of a jeentyłł man,
A feyer poynt for yow he wane,
Desonełł, at the last.'
'Syr,' sche seyd, 'be hevyn kyng,
Tyłł ye me told, I knewe no thyng,
For who ys love yt wase.'
'Desonełł, so mvt I the,
Yt wase for the lowe of the,
That he trovylld so fast.
I warne yow, dowghttyr, be the Rode,
Yt ys for yow bothe good,
Ther to I Red yow trast.'

Forthe sche browght a whyt sted,
As whyt as the flowyr in med,
Ys fytte blac ase slon.
'Leman, haue here thys fole,
That dethe ys dynt schalt þou not thole,

None is better to hold.
I have seen some time in the land,
Whoso had it of my hand,
I fought them I told.

Then Torrent was happy and glad,
The good sword there he had,
The name was Adolake.
A great assembly he made
That lasted all a fortnight,
Whoso would take his meat.
Every man took his leave, as I tell you,
Homeward to go their way,
Everyman took his rest.
Till it befell upon a day,
As they went by the way,
The king spoke to his daughter,

Torrent remains in Provence two weeks before returning to Portugal.

"You shall take heed of a gentleman,
A fair point for you he won,
Desonell, at the last."
"Sir," she said, "by heaven's king,
Till you told me, I knew nothing,
For whose love it was."
"Desonell, so I tell you,
It was for the love of you,
That he travelled so fast.
I warn you, daughter, by the cross,
It is for both your good,
Thereto I advise you trust."

The king of Portugal tells Desonell that Torrent did what he did for her. As a reward, she presents Torrent a white horse, which was a gift to her from the king of Nazareth. She tells him death will not find him while he is in the saddle.

She brought forth a white steed,
As white as the flower in the meadow,
His feet black as sloe.
"My love, have this foal,
That death's strike you shall not endure,

Whyłł thow settyste hyme appon,
And yf thow had persewyd be
And hadyst ned fore to fle,
Fast for to gone.
The kyng of Nazareth sent hym me,
Torrent, I wet-saffe hym on the,
For better love may I none.'

Aftyr-ward vppon a tyd,
Ase the went be the watyres syd,
The kyng and yong Torrent,
The kyng wold fayne, that he ded wer,
And he wyst, in what maner,
How he schuld be schent;
A false lettyr mad the kyng
And dyd messengyres forthe yt bryng,
On the Rever, ase they went,
To Torrent, that was trew ase styłł,
Yf he love Desonełł wyłł,
Get her a facon jent.

Torrent the letter be-gan to Red,
The kyng lestyned & nere yed,
Ase he yt nevyr ad sene.
'Syr,' he seyd, 'what may thys be,
Loo, lord, come ner and see,
A-bowght a facon schene?
I ne wot, so god me sped,
In what lond that they bred.'
The kyng answerd: 'I wene,
In the forrest of Mavdeleyn,
Ther be hawkes, ase I herd seyne,
That byn of lenage clen.'

And than seyd the kyng on-trew:
'Yf thow get hawkys of gret valew,

While you sit upon him,
And if you are pursued
And have need to flee,
Fast for to go.
The king of Nazareth[4] sent him to me,
Torrent, I bestow him on you,
For none better may I love."

Afterward upon a time,
As they went by the waterside,
The king and young Torrent,
The king would rejoice if he were dead,
And he knew, in what manner,
How he should be killed;
The king made a false letter
And had messengers bring it forth,
On the river, as they went,
To Torrent, that was true as steel
If he loved Desonell,
Get her a noble falcon.

The king of Portugal, now dismayed by the growing love between his daughter and Torrent, plots the young man's death. He has a letter given to Torrent asking him to bring a falcon to Desonell as a prize.

The king feigns ignorance of the letter's origins and tells Torrent he believes falcons can be found in the forest of Magdalene, a notably dangerous region. His plan is for Torrent to die in the quest.

Torrent began to read the letter,
The king listened and came near,
As if he'd never seen it.
"Sir," he said, "what may this be,
Look, lord, come near and see,
About a bright falcon?
I know not, so God help me,
In what land they breed."
The king answered, "I know,
In the forest of Magdalene[5],
There are hawks, as I heard said,
That are of clean lineage."

And then the dishonest king said,
"If you get hawks of great value,

Bryng on of them to me!'
Torrent Seyd: 'So god me saue,
Yf yt be-tyd, that I may haue,
At yowr wyłł they schal be.'
Hys squyere bode he thar,
Aftyr hys armor for to far,
In the fyld byddythe he.
They armyd hym in hys wed,
Tho he be-strod a noble sted,
And forthe than Rod hee.

Torrent toke the wey a-geyn
In to the forest of Mawdleyn,
In the wyld-some way;
Berys and apes there founde he,
And wylde bestys great plente,
And lyons where they lay.
Berrys he sawe stondyng
And wyld bestes ther goyng,
Gret lyonys ther he fond.
In a wod that wase tyght,
Yt Drew nere-hand nyght
By dymmynge of the Day,
Harkyn, lordes, to them came wo,
He and hys squyer partyd in two,
Carfułł men then were they.

At the schedyng of a Rome
Eche partyd other frome,
For sothe, ase I vndyrstond.
Torrent toke a dulful wey
Downe in a depe valey
Be-syd a wełł strong.
A lytyłł be fore mydnyght
Of a dragon he had syght,
That grysly wase to fond;

Bring them to me!"
Torrent said, "So God save me,
If it betide, that I may have,
At your will they shall be."
He asked his squire there,
To fetch after his armor,
In the field he waited.
They armed him in his garments,
Then he bestrode a noble steed,
And then forth he rode.

Eager to complete the task, Torrent takes a squire and sets off at once.

The forest of Magdalene is a harsh place filled with wild beasts.

At some point, Torrent and his squire become separated.

Torrent took the way again
Into the forest of Magdalene,
In the wilderness;
Bears and apes he found there,
And a great plenty of wild beasts,
And lions where they lay.
Bears he saw standing
And wild beasts there going,
Great lions there he found.
In a wood that was thick,
It drew near night
By dimming of the day,
Hearken, lords, to them came woe,
He and his squire divided in two,
Sad men then they were.

At the end of a road
Each parted from the other,
For truth, as I understand.
Torrent took a doleful way
Down in a deep valley
Beside a strong spring.
A little before midnight
He had sight of a dragon,
That was grisly to see;

Torrent comes upon a dragon when he realizes his shield and spear are with his squire and he has nothing to fight with but his sword.

He had hym nowght to were,
But hys schyld and hys spere,
That wase in hys squyeres hond.

Torrent knelyd on hys kne,
To Iesu Cryst prayd he:
'Lord, mykyłł of myght,
Syne I wase in meche care,
Let me nevuyr owt of thys world far,
Tyłł I haue take order of knyght.
Ase I ame falsely hether sent,
Wyld-som weyes haue I went,
With fyndes for to fyght.
Now, Iesu, for thy holy name,
Ase I ame but man a-lone,
Than be my helpe to nyght!'

Ase Torrent Iesu gan pray,
He herd the dragon, ther he lay
Vndyr-nethe a clow;
Of and on he wase stronge,
Hys tayle wase VII yerdes long,
That aftyr hyme he drowe;
Hys wyngges wase long and wyght,
To the chyld he toke a flyght
With an howge swowe;
Had he nether schyld ne spere,
But prayd to god, he schold hyme were,
For he wase in dred i-nowe.

On the tayle an hed ther wase,
That byrnyd Bryght as anny glase,
In fyer whan yt was dyght;
A-bowght the schyld he lappyd yt ther,
Thurrow the grace of god almyght.
As the boke of Rome tellys,

He had naught to fight with,
As his shield and his spear,
Were in his squire's hands.

Torrent knelt on his knees,
To Jesus Christ he prayed,
"Lord, full of might,
I have sinned much in grief,
Let me never fare out of this world,
Till I have taken the order of the knight.
As I am falsely sent hither,
Wilderness ways have I gone,
To fight with fiends.
Now, Jesus, for your holy name,
As I am but a man alone,
Be my help tonight!"

As Torrent prayed to Jesus,
He heard the dragon, where he lay
Underneath a bluff;
Off and on he was strong,
His tail was seven yards long,
That he drew after him;
His wings were long and white,
To the child he took flight
With a huge rush;
He had neither shield nor spear,
But prayed to God, he should guard him,
For he was in dread enough.

Torrent prays then engages the dragon in battle. A fierce fight ensues, but Torrent emerges victorious.

On the tail there was a head,
That burned bright as any glass,
In fire when it was ready;
About the chest he wrapped it there,
Through the grace of God almighty.
As the book of Rome tells,

Of hys taylle he cut IIII elles
With hys swerd so bryght.
Than cryed the lothely thyng,
That ałł the dałł be-gan to Ryng,
That hard the gyant wyght.

The gyant seyd: 'I vndyrstond,
There ys sum crystyn man nere hond,
My dragon here I cry.
By hym, that schope bothe watyr and lond,
Ałł that I can se be-fore me stond,
Dere schałł they a-bye!
Me thynkythe, I here my dragon schowt,
I deme, ther be svme dowghtty man hym a-bowght,
I trow, to long I ly.
Yf I dwełł in my pyłł of ston,
And my cheff-foster were gone,
A false myster were I!'

Be the gyant wase Redy dyght,
Torrent had slayne the dragon Ryght;
Thus gan god hyme scheld.
To the mownteyne he toke the wey
To Rest hyme, ałł that day,
He had myster, to be kyld.
Tyłł the day be-gan to spryng,
Fowllys gan myrre to syng
Bothe in frethe and in feld.
Leve we now of Torrent thore
And speke we of thys squyer more:
Iesu hys sole fro hełł shyld!

Hys squyer Rod ałł nyght
In a wod, that wase fułł tyght,
With meche care and gret fare,
For to seke hys lord Torrent,

Of his tail he cut four pieces
With his sword so bright.
Then cried the loathsome thing,
That all the dell began to ring,
That heard the giant creature.

The giant said, "I understand,
There is some Christian man near at hand,
I hear my dragon cry.
By him, that shapes water and land,
All that I can see before me stand,
Dear shall they buy!
I think I hear my dragon shout,
I deem, there be some brave man about him,
In truth, so long as I live.
If I dwell in my pile of stone,
And my chief child were gone,
A false master am I!"

A giant lives nearby and hears the cry of the dragon. He rushes to save his pet but is too late.

By the time the giant was ready,
Torrent had slain the dragon;
Thus did God shield him.
To the mountain he took the way
To rest, all that day,
He had need to rest.
Till the day began to spring,
Fowls sang merrily
Both in forest and in field.
We will now leave Torrent there
And speak of his squire more,
Jesus shield his soul from hell!

Torrent leaves to rest after slaying the dragon and is not there when the giant arrives.

His squire rode all night
In a wood that was very thick,
With much grief and great fear ,
To seek his lord Torrent,

That wyghtly wase frome hyme sent,
And he wyst nevyr whethyr ne whar.
He Durst neuyr cry ne schuot,
For wyld bestes were hym a-bowght
In the holttes hare;
A lytyl whyłł be-fore the day
He toke in to a Ryde-wey
Hyme self to meche care.

Forthe he Rod, I vndyrstond,
Tyłł he an hey wey ford,
With-owtyn any Delite,
Also fast ase he myght fare,
Fore berrys and apys, þat ther ware,
Lest they wold hym byght.
The sone a-Rose and schone bryght,
Of a castyłł he had a syght,
That wase bothe feyer and whyte . . . .

The gyant him se, & ny yed,
And seyd: 'Fellow, so god me sped,
Thow art welcom to me:
What dost thow here in my forest?'
'Lord, to seke an hawkys nest,
Yff yt yowr wyl be.'
'The be-hovythe to ley a wede.'
To an oke he hym led:
Gret Ruthe yt wase to se.
In IV quarteres he hym drowe,
And euery quarter vppon a bowe;
Lord, soche weys toke hee!

Ase Torrent in the movnteyn dyd ly,
Hym thowght, he hard a Reufułł cry;
Gret fere ther hyme thowght.
'Seynt Marre,' seyd the chyld so fre,

That was indeed sent from him,
And he knew not whither nor where.
He dared never cry nor shout,
For wild beasts were about him
In the foul woods;
A little while before the day
He took into a roadway
By himself with much grief.

Torrent's squire travels the woods alone before coming to a roadway which leads him to the giant's castle.

Forth he rode, I understand,
Till he came to a highway,
Without any delay,
As fast as he might fare,
Before bears and apes, that were there,
Lest they would bite him.
The sun rose and shone bright,
Of a castle he had sight,
That was both fair and white . . . .

The giant saw him and went near,
And said, "Fellow, so God help me,
That are welcome to me.
What are you doing here in my forest?"
"Lord, to seek a hawk's nest,
If it be your will."
"It behooves you to lay a payment."
To an oak he led him,
Great pity it was to see.
In four quarters he drew him,
And every quarter upon a bough;
Lord, such ways took he!

The giant finds the squire and brutally quarters him, hanging the parts from a tree.

Torrent hears the squire's cries and rides to the source, finding the murdered man.

As Torrent lay in the mountain,
He thought he heard a rueful cry;
Great fear there he thought.
"Saint Mary," said the child so free,

'Wher euyr my jentyłł squyer myght be,
That I with me to wod browght?
On he dyd hys harnes a-geyne
And worthe on hys sted, serteyne,
And thetherward he sowght.
And wot yow wyłł, I vndyrstond,
In fowre quartyres he hym fownd,
For other wyse wase yt nowght.

The gyant lenyd to a tre
And be-hyld Torrent so free,
For sothe, ase I yow seye.
Thys fend wase ferly to fyght,
Rochense, seythe the boke, he hyght,
Ther wase a dredfułł fraye.
To the chyld than gan he smyght:
'A theff, yeld the asttyt,
As fast as thow may!'
'What,' seyd Torrent, 'art thow wood?
God, that Dyed on the Rood,
Geff the evyłł happe thys day!'

He Rawght Torrent soche a Rowght,
Hys steddes brayne he smot owte,
So mykyłł he be-gan.
Torrent tho a good sped
Ase fast a-bowte an eche yede;
Ase swefte ase he myght, he Ran.
He gathyred svm of hys gere,
Bothe hys schyld and hys spere;
Nere hym yod he than.
Bacward than be a brow3
Twenty fote he gard hyme goo,
Thus erthe on hym he wane.

Yt solasyd Torrant then,

"Wherever might be my gentle squire,
That I brought with me to this wood?"
He put his harness on again
And mounted his steed, certain,
And thither he sought.
And know you well, I understand,
In four quarters he found him,
For otherwise was it not.

The giant leaned on a tree
And beheld Torrent so free,
For truth, as I tell you.
This fiend was dangerous to fight,
Rochense, says the book, he was called,
There was a dreadful fray.
To the child then he smote,
"A thief, go down,
As fast as you may!"
"What," Torrent said, "are you mad?
God, that died on the cross,
Give you bad luck this day!"

Torrent engages the giant in battle. His horse is quickly killed.

The two fight for hours, neither gaining the advantage until Torrent forces the giant to stumble down to the base of a valley.

He wrought Torrent such a blow,
His steed's brains he smote out,
So strong he began.
Torrent though at good speed
As fast about each went;
As swift as he might, he ran.
He gathered some of his gear,
Both his shield and his spear;
Near him he went then.
Backward then was a brow
Twenty foot he made him go,
Thus he won earth on him.

It solaced Torrent then,

When he sawe hyme bacward ren
Downe be a movnteyn of Perowne,
Stomlyng thurrow frythe and fen,
Tyłł he com to a depe glen,
Ther myght non hym stere.
Torrent wase glad and folowyd fast,
And hys spere on hyme he brast,
Good Adyloke yed hyme nere.
The fynd in the watyr stod,
He fawte a-geyn, ase he were wod,
Ałł þe day in fere.

Tho nere hond wase the day gone,
Torrent wase so werry than
That on hys kne he kneld:
'Helpe, god, that ałł may!
Dosonełł, haue good day!'
Fro hym he cest hys schyld.
Iesu wold not, he were slayne,
To hym he sent a schowyr of Rayne,
Torrent fułł wyłł yt keld.
The fynd saw, he wase ny mate,
Owt of the watyr he toke the gate,
He thowght to wyne the fyld.

Thoo wase Torrent ffresse and good;
Nere the fynd sore he stod,
Cryst hym saue and see!
The fynd fawt with an yron staff,
The fyrst stroke, to hym he gaffe,
He brast hys schyld on thre.
Torrent vndyr hys staff Rane,
To the hart he baryd hym than,
And lothely cry gane he.
To the grownd he fełł ase tyght,
And Torrent gan hys hed of-smyght,

When he saw him run backwards
Down the mountain of Perrown,
Stumbling through forest and fen,
Till he came to a deep glen,
There might nothing stir him.
Torrent was glad and followed fast,
And his spear on him he burst,
Good Adolake went near him
The fiend in the water stood,
They fought again, as if they were mad,
All the day together.

Though the day was nearly gone,
Torrent was so weary then
That on his knee he knelt,
"Help, God, all that may!
Desonell, have good day!"
From him he cast his shield.
Jesus would not, he were slain,
To him he sent a shower of rain,
It fully cooled Torrent.
The fiend saw, he was nearly defeated,
Out of the water he took the path
He thought to win the field.

> After a long fight Torrent pauses and prays for help. A cooling rain falls that refreshes him and he continues the battle. He is able to deal the giant a mortal blow to the heart before cutting off his head.

Though was Torrent refreshed and good;
Near the fiend sorely he stood,
Christ save him and see!
The fiend fought with an iron staff,
The first stroke, to him he gave,
He burst his shield in three.
Torrent under his staff ran,
To the heart he thrust him then,
And fiercely he cried.
To the ground he fell,
And Torrent smote off his head,

And thus he wynnythe the gre.
Torrent knelyd on the grownd
And thankyd god þat ylke stownd,
That soche grace hyme send.
Thus II journeys in thys woo
With hys handes slow he gyantys too,
That meny a man hathe schent.
Torrent forthe frome hyme þan yod,
And met hyme XXIIII fotte,
Ther he lay on the bent.
Hedles he left hym there,
Howt of the fyld the hed he bare
And to the castełł he went.

To thys castełł he gan far;
Ther fond he armor and other gare,
A swerd, that wase bryght.
To the towre he toke the wey,
Ther the gyantes bed lay,
That Rychyly wase dyght.
At the beddes hed he fond
A swerd, worthe an Erllys lond,
That meche wase of myght.
On the pomełł yt wase wret,
Fro a prynce yt wase get,
Mownpolyardnus he hyght.

The sarten to sey with-owt lese,
A scheff-chambyr he hym ches,
Tyłł on the morrow day.
To the stabułł tho he yed,
There he fond a nobyłł sted,
Wase comely whyt and grey.
The gyanttes hed gan he take,
And the dragonnys wold he not forsake,
And went forthe on hys wey.

And thus he won the prize.
Torrent knelt on the ground
And thanked God that same time,
That he sent him such grace.
Thus two journeys in this way
With his hands he slayed two giants,
That had killed many men.
Torrent went forth from him then,
And measured him twenty-four feet,
Where he lay on the grass.
Headless he left him there,
Out of the field the head he bore
And to the castle he went.

To this castle he fared;
There he found armor and other gear,
A sword, that was bright.
To the tower he took the way,
There the giant's bed lay
That was richly adorned.
At the bed's head he found
A sword, worth an earl's land,
That was very mighty.
On the pommel it was written,
From a prince it was gotten,
Mounpolyardnus he was called.

> Torrent enters the giant's castle and finds his treasure, including a mighty sword engraved with the name Mounpolyardnus.
>
> After spending the night in the castle, Torrent takes a horse from the stable and rides home to Portugal.

Certainly, without lie,
A chief chamber he chose,
Till on the following day.
To the stable he then went,
There he found a noble steed,
That was comely white and gray.
The giant's head he took,
And the dragon's would he not forsake,
And went forth on his way.

He left mor good in that sale
Than wase with in alł Portynggalł,
Ther ase the gyant laye.

Tho he Rod bothe Day and nyght,
Tyłł he come to a castełł bryght,
Ther ys lord gan dwełł.
The kyng ys gone to the gate,
Torrent on kne he fond ther at,
Schort tałł for to tełł.
'Haue thow thys in thyn hond:
No nother hawkys ther I fond
At Mawdlenys wełł.'
The kyng quod: 'Ase so haue I blyse,
Torrent, I trow, sybbe ys
To the dewełł of hełł! . . . .

'Here be syd dwellythe won on lond,
Ther ys no knyght, hys dynt may stond,
So stronge he ys in dede!'
'Syr,' he sayd, 'fore sen Iame,
What ys the gyantes name,
So Euyr good me sped?'
'Syr,' he seyd, 'so mvt I the,
Slogus of Fuolles, thus hyte hee,
That wyt ys vndyr wede.' . . . .

Lytyłł and mykyłł, lese and more,
Wondyr on the heddes thore,
That Torrent had browght whome.
The Lordes seyd 'Be sen Myhełł!
Syr kyng, but ye love hyme wyłł,
To yow yt ys gret schame!'
Torent ordeynyd prystes fyve,
To syng for hys squyerys lyve,
And menythe hym by name.

He left more good in that hall
Than was with all in Portugal,
There as the giant lay.

Then he rode both day and night,
Till he came to a castle bright,
There his lord did dwell.
The king went to the gate,
Torrent on his knee he found there,
A short tale to tell.
"Have you this in your hand,
No other hawks there I found
At Magdalene's well[6]."
The king said, "As so I have bliss,
Torrent, my faith, is like
To the devil in hell! . . . .

Torrent tells the king he was unable to find a falcon for Desonell. While the nobles of Portugal marvel at the severed head of the giant and his dragon, the king tells Torrent of another giant that may need killing.

"There is said to dwell one on land,
There is no knight, his blow may stand,
So strong he is in deed!"
"Sir," he said, "before Saint James[7],
What is the giant's name,
So ever God give me success?"
"Sir," he said, "So I tell you,
Slogus of Fuolles, thus he is called,
That is white under his clothes." . . . .

Little and much, less and more,
Wondered on the heads there,
That Torrent had brought home.
The lords said, "By Saint Michael!
Sir king, but you love him well,
To you it is a great shame!"
Torrent ordained priests five,
To sing for his squire's life,
And mention him by name.

Therfor the lady whyt ase swane
To Torrant, here lord, sche went than,
Here hert wase to hyme tane.

Lettyrres come ther withalle
To the kyng of Portynggałł,
To ax hys dowghttyr Derre,
Fro the kyng of Eragon,
To wed her to hys yongeest son,
The lady, that ys so clere.
For Torrent schuld not her haue,
For hyme fyrst he here gafe,
To the messenger,
And hys way fast ageyn dyd pase,
Whyle Torrent an huntyng wase,
Ther of schuld he not be were.

On a mornyng, ther ase he lay,
The kyng to the quene gan sey:
'Madame, for cherryte,
Thow art oftyn hold wyse;
Now wołł ye tełł me yowr deuyce,
How I may governe me:
The Ryche kyng hathe to me sent,
For to aske my dowghttyr gente
That ys so feyer and fre.'
'Syr,' sche Seyd, 'so god me saue,
I Red yow let Torent her haue,
For best worthy ys he.'

He sayd: 'Madame, were that feyer,
To make an erlles sone myn Eyer?
I wiłł not, by sen Iame!
There he hathe done maystres thre,
Yt ys hys swerd, yt ys not he,
For Hatheloke ys ys name.'

Therefore the lady white as a swan
To Torrent, her lord, she went then,
Her heart was taken by him.

Letters came there withal,
To the king of Portugal,
To ask for his daughter dear,
From the king of Aragon[8],
To wed her to his youngest son,
The lady, that is so bright.
For Torrent should not have her,
For him first he gave her,
To the messenger,
And his way fast again did pass,
While Torrent was hunting,
Thereof he should not be aware.

A letter arrives asking the king of Portugal to wed Desonell to the prince of Aragon. While Torrent is out hunting, the king agrees to the marriage proposal and sends messengers to Aragon.

On a morning, there as he lay,
The king said to the queen,
"Madame, for charity,
You are often wise;
Now will you tell my your desire,
How I may govern me,
The rich king has sent to me,
To ask for my gentle daughter
That is so fair and free."
"Sir," she said, "so God save me,
I advise you let Torrent have her,
For he is most worthy."

The king consults the queen about Desonell, telling her about Aragon's proposal. The queen favors Torrent, but the king refuses to make the son of a mere earl his heir. He says Torrent's victories are owed more to his sword than his prowess. The queen warns him that he had already told Torrent he would win Desonell for killing the giant, and to deny him his reward will only bring shame.

He said, "Madame, were that fair,
To make an earl's son my heir?"
I will not, by Saint James!
There he has done three services,
It is his sword, it is not he,
For Adolake is its name."

'Lord, he myght fułł wyłł sped,
A knyghtes dowghttyr wase hyme bed,
Ase whyt ase walles bane;
And yf ye warne hyme Desonełł,
All that ther of here tełł,
Ther of wyłł speke schame.'

'Madam, vnto thys tyd
There lythe a gyant here be-syd,
That many a man hathe slayne.
I schałł hyght hym my dowghttyr dere,
To fyght with that fyndes fere,
Thus he holdythe hyme in trayne.
But I schałł make myn commnant so,
That there schałł non with hyme go,
Neyther squyer ne swayne.'
'Syr,' sche seyd, 'so mvt I the,
So sore be-stad hathe he be,
And wyłł commyn a-geyne!'

Tho the belles be-gan to Ryng,
Vpe Rose that Ryche kyng,
And the lady so fre,
And aftyr-ward they went to mase,
Ase the law of holy chyrge wase,
With notes and solemnyte.
Trompettys on the wałł gan blowe,
Knyghtes semlyd on a Rowe,
Gret joy wase to see.
Torrent a syd bord began,
The squyeres nexte hym than,
That good knyghtes schuld be.

Ase they sat a-myddes the mete,
The kyng wold not foreget;
To Torrent the kyng gan sey,

"Lord, he might full well succeed,
A knight's daughter was his offer,
As white as whale's bone;
And if it were not Desonell,
All that thereof here tell,
Thereof will speak shame."

The king tells the queen he will send Torrent to fight another giant alone, and if he succeeds this final time, he will grant him Desonell's hand, though he is certain Torrent will be killed.

The queen says he is wrong, and Torrent will return again victorious.

"Madam, unto this time
There lies a giant here beside,
That has slain many a man.
I shall give him my daughter dear,
To fight with that fiend's company,
Thus he hold him in a trap.
But I shall make my commandment so,
That none shall go with him there,
Neither squire nor attendant."
"Sir," she said, "So I must,
So sorely bestead has he been,
And will come again!"

Then the bells began to ring,
Up rose that rich king,
And the lady so free,
And afterward they went to mass,
As was the law of the holy church,
With notes and solemnity.
Trumpets on the wall blew,
Knights assembled in a row,
Great joy it was to see.
Torrent went to a side board,
The squires next to him then,
That good knights should be.

As they sat amidst the meat,
The king would not forget;
To Torrent the king began to say,

He seyd: ' Torrent, so god me saue,
Thow woldes fayne my dowghttyr haue
And hast lovyd her many a day.'
'Ye, be trouthe,' seyd Torrent than,
'And yf þat I were a Ryche man,
Ryght gladly, par ma fay!'
'Yf thow durst for her sake
A poynt of armys vndyrtake,
Thow broke her wełł fore ay!'

'Ye,' seyd Torrent, 'ar I ga,
Sekyrnes ye schałł me ma
Of yowr dowghttyr hend,
And aftyrward my ryghtys,
Be-fore XXVII knyghtes.' . . . .
And ałł were Torrent es frende.
'Now, good seris,' gan Torrant sey,
'Bere wittnes her of som Daye,
A-geyne yf god me send!'

Torrent seyd: 'So mvt I the
Wyst I, where my jorney schold be,
Thether I wolde me dyght.'
The kyng gaff hyme an answere:
'In the lond of Calabur ther
Wonnythe a gyant wyhte,
And he ys bothe strong and bold,
Slochys he hyght, I the told,
God send the that waye Ryght!'
Than quod Torrent : 'Haue good day,
And, or I come a-geyn, I schałł asay,
Whether the fynd can fyght.'

Tho wold he no lenger a-byde,
He toke ys wey for to Ryde
On a sted of gret valewe.

He said, "Torrent, so God save me,
You would gladly have my daughter
And have loved her many a day."
"Yes, it is true," Torrent said then,
"And if that I were a rich man,
Right gladly, by my faith!"
"If you dare for her sake
A task of arms undertake,
You will have her forever!"

The next day the king tells Torrent of a giant in the land of Calabria. Torrent swears to kill the giant and the king promises, in front of all his knights, to give him Desonell in marriage if he succeeds, though he has already arranged for her to be wed to the prince of Aragon. Torrent makes ready and departs.

"Yet," Torrent said, "before I go,
Certain you shall make me
Of your daughter's hand,
And afterward my rights,
Before twenty-seven knights." . . . .
And all were Torrent's friends.
"Now good sirs," Torrent said,
"Bear witness here of some day,
Again if God sends me!"

Torrent said, "So I must,
Know, where my journey should be,
Thither I will prepare myself."
The king gave him an answer,
"In the land of Calabria[9] there
Lives a white giant,
And he is both strong and bold,
Slogus he is called, I told you,
God send you that way quick!"
Then Torrent said, "Have good day,
And, before I come again, I shall test,
Whether the fiend can fight."

Then he would no longer wait,
He took his way to ride
On a steed of great value.

In to a chambyr he gas,
Hys leue of Desonełł he tas,
Sche wepte, ałł men myght Rewe;
He seyd: 'Lady, be styłł!
I schałł come a-geyn the tyłł,
Thurrow helpe of Marry trewe.'
Thus he worthe on a stede.
In hys wey Cryst hyme sped,
Fore he yt no thyng knewe!

He toke hym a Redy wey,
Thurrow Pervyns he toke the wey,
As hys Iorney fełł.
Tyłł the castełł Be the See,
An hy stret heldythe hee,
Ther the kyng dyd dwelle.
To the porter he gan seye:
'Wynd in, fellow, I the pray,
And thy lord than tełł,
Pray hym, on won nyght in hys sale
To harburrow Torrent of Portynggałł,
Yf yt Bee ys wiłł!'

The porter Dyd hys commandment,
To the kynge he ys wente
And knelyd vppon ys kne:
'God blyse þe, lord,
In thy sale! Torrent of Portynggale
Thus sendythe me to the;
He praythe yow, yf ye myght,
To harburrow hym thys won nyght,
Yf yowr wiłł yt bee.'
The kyng swere be hym,
þat dyed on tre:
'There ys no man in crystyante
More welcome to me!'

Into a chamber he went,
He took his leave of Desonell.
She wept, all men might rue;
He said, "Lady, be still!
I shall come again to you,
Through the help of Mary true."
Thus he mounted on a steed.
In his way Christ guided him,
For he knew nothing!

He took the prudent way,
Through Provence he took the way,
As his journey fell.
Till the castle by the sea,
A high street held he,
There the king did dwell.
To the porter he said,
"Go in, fellow, I pray you,
And tell your lord,
Pray he, for one night in his hall,
To harbor Torrent of Portugal,
If it be his will!"

Torrent arrives at a castle in Provence and is welcomed by the king there.

The porter did is commandment,
To the king he went
And knelt upon his knee,
"God bless you, lord,
In your hall! Torrent of Portugal,
Thus sent me to you;
He prays you, if you might,
Harbor him this one night,
If it be your will."
The king swore by him,
That died on the tree
"There is no man in Christendom

The kyng a-Rose and to the gat yod,
Lordes and other knyghtes good,
That were glad of hys commyng.
In to the hale he hyme browght,
Ryche met spare they nowght,
Be-fore Torrent fore to bryng.
'Syr,' sayd the kyng, 'I pray the,
Where be thy men off armys free,
That with the schuld leng?'
'Syr, to a lord I mvst Ryde,
My squyer hongythe be my syde,
No man schałł with me wend.'

'Syr,' seyd the kyng, 'I pray the,
Where schałł thy ded of armys bee,
Yf yt be thy wyłł?'
'Syr,' he seyd, 'vttyrly, At Calabur, sekyrly,
I ame ałł Redy ther tyłł
With a squyer, þat wiłł can Ryde;
Fast be the see Sydde
Schuld we pley owur fyle;
And wot ye wyłł and vndyrstond,
Ther schałł no knyght come nere hond
Fore dred of denttes yłł.'

The kynge seyd: 'Be goddes ore,
I Rede, þat þou come not thore,
Fore why, I wyłł the seye:
Meche folke of that contre
Come hether for sokor of me,
Bothe be nyght and day;
There ys a gyant of gret Renowne,
He dystrowythe bothe sete and towyn
And ałł þat euyr he may;
And ase the boke of Rome dothe tełł,

More welcome to me!"
The king arose and went to the gate,
Lords and other knights good,
That were glad of his coming.
Into the hall he brought them,
Rich meat they did not spare,
To bring before Torrent.
"Sir," the king said, "I pray you,
Where be your men of arms free,
That should dwell with you?"
"Sir, to a lord I must ride,
My squire was hung by my side,
No man shall go with me."

At a feast in the castle Torrent recounts the death of his squire. He tells the king he travels alone to Calabria to slay a giant.

"Sir," the king said, "I pray you,
Where shall your deed of arms be,
If it be your will?"
"Sir," he said, "Utterly, at Calabria, certainly,
I am ready to go there till
With a squire, that can ride;
Fast by the seaside
Should we play our fill;
And know you will and understand,
No knight shall come near at hand
For dread of ill blows."

The king said, "By God's favor,
I advise, that you don't go there,
Because, I will say to you,
Many folk of that country
Come hither for succor from me,
Both night and day;
There is a giant of great renown,
He destroys both seat and town
And all that ever he may;
And as the book of Rome tells,

He wase get of the dewełł of hełł,
As hys moder on slepe lay.'

The kyng Seyd: 'Be seynt Adryan,
I Rede, a nother Jentyłł mane
Be there and haue the gre:
I haue a dowghttyr, þat ys me dere,
Thow schalt here wed to thy fere,
And, yf yt thy wyll be,
Two duchyes in londe
I wille geve here in hande.'
'Gramarcy, syr,' sayd he,
'With my tonge so haue I wrowght,
To breke my day than wiłł I nowght,
Nedys me behovythe ther to bee.'

'In goddes name,' the kyng gane sayne,
'Iesu send the wiłł a-geyne,
Lord so mekyłł of myghte!'
Menstrelles was them a-monge,
Trompettes, harpys, and myrre songe,
Delycyous nottis on hyght.
When tyme was, to bed they wente;
On the morrow Rose Torrente
And toke leve of kyng and knyght
And toke a Redy weyye,
Be a see syd as yt laye,
God send hym gattes Ryght!

A hye stret hathe he nome,
In to Calabur he ys come
With in to days ore III;
Soo come ther folkes hym a-geyne,
Fast folloyng with cart and wayne,
Fro-ward the sytte.
'Dere god!' seyd Torrent nowe,

He was begot of the devil of hell,
As his mother lay asleep."

The king said, "By Saint Adrian[10],
I advise, another gentle complaint
Be there and have the prize.
I have a daughter, that is dear to me,
You shall wed her,
And if it is your will,
Two duchies in the land
I will give her in hand."
"Many thanks, sir," he said,
"With my tongue so I have wrought,
To break my day than will I not,
Needs behoove me there to be."

The king warns Torrent about the vicious nature of the giant and offers him two duchies and his own daughter as a reward if he succeeds in killing him.

"In God's name," the king said,
"Jesus send you will again,
Lord so much of might!"
Minstrels were among them,
Trumpets, harps, and merry song,
Delicious notes were played.
When the time was, to bed they went;
On the morrow Torrent rose
And took leave of king and knight
And took a ready way,
By a seaside as it lay,
God sent him right!"

He came to a highway,
Into Calabria he came
Within two or three days;
Soon folks came to him again,
Fast following with cart and wagon,
From the city.
"Dear God!" Torrent said now,

'Leve folkes, what Eyllythe yow,
Soo fast fore to flee?'
'There ys a gyante here be-syde,
In ale thys covntre fare and wyde
No mane on lyve levythe hee.'

'Dere god,' sayd Torrant thane,
'Where schałł I fynd that lothly man?'
Ther they answerd hym anone:
'In a castyłł be-syd the see,
Slongus, soo hyght hee,
Many a man had he slone.
We wot wiłł wher he doth ly:
Be-fore the cyte of Hungry;
He wiłł not thens gone,
Tyłł he haue the Ryche kyng
To hys presone for to bryngg,
To be lord of hyme self a-lone.'

Tho wold he no lenger a-byd,
But to the sytte gan he Ryde,
As fast as he myght fare;
Here barys fełł and broke downe,
And the gattes of gret Renowne
Stondyng ałł baree.
Men of armys stond hyme a-geyne,
Mo than fyfty had he slayne
With gryme wounddes and sare.
When Torrent of hym had a syght,
Thowe Desonełł be neuyr so bryght,
He will Reue hym hys chaffar.

Torrent in the storrope stod
And prayd to god, þat dyed on Rode:
'Lord, ase thow schalt ale wyld at wyle,
Gyff me grace to wyn the fyld,

"Dear folks, what troubles you,
To flee so fast before?"
"There is a giant here beside,
In all this country fair and wide
He leaves no man alive."

"Dear God," Torrent said then
"Where shall I find that terrible man?"
There they answered him at once,
"In a castle beside the sea,
Slogus, so he is called,
Many a man he has slain.
We know where he lies,
Before the city of Hungary[11];
He will not thence go,
Till he has the rich king
Brought to his prison,
To be lord by himself alone."

After some days Torrent comes to a roadway leading into Calabria. He meets fleeing citizens who tell him the giant has taken the city of Hungary where he seeks to imprison the king and rule the land.

Then he would no longer abide,
But to the city he did ride,
As fast as he might fare;
Here barriers fell and broke down,
And the gates of great renown
Stood all bare.
Men of arms stood against him,
More than fifty he had slain
With grim wounds and pain.
When Torrent had sight of him,
Though Desonell was never so bright,
He will rue his business.

Torrent arrives at the city gates and finds many dead. He pauses to pray for victory.

Torrent stood in his stirrup
And prayed to God, that died on the cross,
"Lord, as you shall wield all the world,
Give me grace to win the field,

That thys lothly fynd hym yeld A-non to me tyłł!
A man schałł But onnys Dyee,
I wiłł fyght, whiłł I may Dryee.'
He mad cher nobyłł.
When he had Iesu prayd of grace,
He wyscheyd hyme a battełł plase,
Ther as hym lyst welle.

Torrent hys spere a-say be-gane,
Bothe schyld and spere than,
That they were sekyr and good.
Aftyr þat, with in a throwe,
Hys good horne gane he blowe.
The gyant sawe, wher he stodde:
Slonges of Flonthus staryd than;
Quod Torrent: 'Yf thow be a gentyłł man
Or come of gentyłł blod,
Let thy beytyng and thy Ermyght be,
And come prove thy strenghe on me,
Therfor I sowght the, be the Rodde.'

The gyant sayd: 'Be the Roode,
Dewełł of hełł send the fode,
Hether to seche me:
By the nose I schałł the wryng,
Thow berdles gadlyng,
That ałł hełł schałł thow see!'
The wey than to hym he toke
And on hys bake he bare a croke,
Wase X fot long and thre;
And thow he neuer so gret war,
Torrent thowght not fare to fare,
Tyłł wone of them ded bee.

Thoo wold Torrent no lenger byd,
Tyłł the theff gan he Ryde,

That this terrible fiend yield at once to me!
A man shall but once die,
I will fight, while I may try."
He made noble cheer.
When he had prayed of Jesus' grace,
He wished him a battle place,
There as he knew well.

Torrent began to test his spear,
Both shield and spear then,
That they were sound and good.
After that, within a short time,
He blew his good horn.
The giant saw, where he stood,
Slogus of Fuolles stared then;
Torrent said, "If you be a gentleman
Or come of gentle blood,
Let your beating and your past feats be,
And come prove your strength on me,
Therefore I sought you, by the cross."

Torrent readies his weapons and blows his battle horn to attract the giant.

The giant said, "By the cross,
The devil of hell sent you young child,
Hither to seek me.
I shall wring you by the nose,
You beardless vagabond,
That all hell shall you see!"
The way then to him he took
And on his back he bore a crook,
That was ten foot long and three;
And though he was never so great,
Torrent thought not to fare far,
Till one of them was dead.

Then Torrent would no longer wait,
To the wretch he rode,

Ase fast ase euyr he may.
The theff had non ey but on,
Soche sawe I neuer none,
Neyther be nyght nor be day.
Thurrow goddes helpe and sent Awsden
The spere throw ye and herne gan ren.
God send hym the Ryght wey;
Than the theff be-gane to Rore.
Ałł that in the sytte wore,
Ouyr the wallys they laye.

Thow the fyndes ey were owte,
Fast he leyd hym a-bowte
Ałł þat somyrres nyght;
He set ys backe to an hyłł,
That Torrent schuld not come hym tyłł,
So meche þat theff covd of fyght.
He bled so sore, I vndyrstond,
Hys croke fełł owt of hys hond,
Hys dethe to hyme ys dyght.
Torrent to hyme Rane with a spere,
Thurrow the body he gan hym bere,
Thus helpe hym god of myght.

Ałł that in the sytte were,
Mad fułł nobiłł chere,
That thys fynd wase Dedde.
Forthe they Ran with stavys of tre,
Torrent seyd: 'So mvt I the,
Kepe hole hys hed!
Yf yt be broke, so god me sped,
Yt ys wyłł the worse to lede'.
They dyd ase he hem bede,
Mo than thre hunderd on a throng
Yt ys solas Euyr a-mong
Whan that he was dede.

As fast as ever he may.
The scoundrel had but one eye,
Such as I never saw one,
Neither by night nor by day.
Through God's help and Saint Augustine[12]
The spear through the eye and brains ran.
God sent him the right way;
Then the wretch began to roar.
All that in the city were
Over the walls they lay.

The fight commences. The giant has but one good eye and Torrent quickly puts it out to blind his enemy completely.

The battle is long. Eventually, Torrent runs the fiend through with his spear, killing him.

Though the fiend's eye was out,
Fast he led him about
All that summer's night;
He set his back to a hill,
That Torrent should not come to him,
So much that scoundrel knew of fighting.
He bled so sorely, I understand,
His crook fell out of his hand,
His death to him came readily.
Torrent ran to him with a spear,
Through his body he bore it,
Thus help him God of might.

All who were in the city,
Made full noble cheer,
That this fiend was dead.
They ran forth with tree staves,
Torrent said, "So I must,
Keep whole his head!
If it is broken, so God help me,
It is well the worse to the people."
They did as he bid them,
More than three hundred in a throng
There was solace ever among
When he was dead.

The citizens rejoice. Torrent commands that the giant's head be preserved for his prize.

Than the kyng of Calaber ayen hym went,
Torrent be the hond he hent,
To the hałł he gan hym lede
And comaundid squiers two,
Of hys harnes for to do
And cloth hym in another wede.
Waytes on the wałł gan blowe,
Knyghtis assemled on a Rowe,
And sith to the deyse they yede;
'Sir,' quod the kyng, 'of whens are ye?'
'Of Portingale, sir,' said he,
'I com heder, to sech my dede.'

Fułł curtesly the kyng gan say
To Torrent on the oþure day:
'Wyłł ye wend with me
A litułł here be-side to passe,
There as the Geauntes dwelling was
His maner now for to see?'
To the castełł gan they gone,
Richer saw they never none,
Better myght none be.
'Sir,' he said, 'be god ałł-myȝt,
For thou hym slew, þat it dight,
I vouche it saue on the.

'I yeve yt the, sir, of my hond,
And there-to, an erledome of my lond,
For soth, ye shałł it haue;
Omage thou shalte none nor ffyne,
But euer more to the and thyne,
Frely, so god me saue!'
Lordys, and ye liston wold,
What was clepud the riche hold:
The castełł of Cardon, by sawe.

Then the king of Calabria went to him again,
He took Torrent by the hand,
To the hall he led him
And commanded two squires,
To do up his harness
And clothe him in another garment.
Guards on the wall blew,
Knights assembled in a row,
And after to the dais they went;
"Sir," the king said, "of whence are you?"
"Of Portugal, sir," he said,
"I come hither to seek my deed."

Courteously the king said
To Torrent on the other day,
"Will you go with me
A little here beside the pass,
Where the giant's dwelling was
To see his manner now?"
To the castle they went,
They never saw richer,
None might be better.
"Sir," he said, "by God almighty,
For you slew him, that is rewarded,
I vouchsafe it on you.

The grateful king of Calabria gives Torrent the giant's castle as a gift and tells him he and his descendants may live there forever and never pay any tribute.

"I give it to you, sir, of my hand,
And thereto, an earldom of my land,
For truth, you shall have it;
You shall pay no homage,
But ever more to you and yours,
Freely, so God save me!"
Lords, and you will listen,
What the rich hold was called,
The castle of Cardon[13].

Two days or thre dwellith he thare
And sith he takythe leve to ffare,
Both at knyght and knave.

By the kyng of Pervens he gan gane,
That he had oute of preson i-tane
His son vppon a day.
Gentilmen were blith and ffayn,
That he in helth was comyn agayn,
That they myght with hym play.
There of herd he, sertaynle,
That Desonełł wedid shold be
With an vncouth Ray.
And listonyth, lordis, of a chaunce,
Howe he lefte his countenaunce
And takyth hym armes gay!

By-fore the kyng he fełł on kne:
'Good lord,' he said, 'for charite,
Yeve me order of knyght!
I wott wełł, leryd are ye,
My lordys doughter shałł wed be
To a man off myght.'
'Sir,' he said, 'I trow, she mone
To the prynce off Aragon,
By this day sevynnyght.
Swith,' he seith, 'that this be done,
That thou be there and wyn thy shone,
Gete the armes bryght.'

Sir Torrent ordenyth hym a sheld,
It was ryche in euery ffeld,
Listonyth, what he bare:
On aȝure a squier off gold,
Richely bett on mold;
Listonyth, what he ware:

Two days or three he stayed there,
And after he took leave to fare,
Both of knight and knave.

To the king of Provence he went again,
That he had taken out of prison
His son upon a day.
Gentlemen were blithe and fain,
That he in health came again,
That they might play with him.
There he heard, certainly,
That Desonell wedded should be
With an unknown king.
And listen, lords, of a chance,
How he left his countenance
And took up bright arms!

After a few days Torrent leaves Calabria for Portugal. Along the way he stops in Provence where he learns from the king there Desonell is to be wedded to the prince of Aragon.

Torrent asks the king of Provence to "win his shoes," i.e., knight him.

He fell on his knee before the king,
"Good lord," he said, "for charity,
Give me the order of the knight!
I know well, learned are you,
My lord's daughter shall be wed
To a man of might."
"Sir," he said, "I know, she must
To the prince of Aragon,
By this day seven nights.
Promptly," he said, "that this be done,
That you be there and win your shoes,
Get you arms bright."

Sir Torrent got a shield,
It was rich in every way,
Listen, what he bore:
On azure a square of gold,
With a richly engraved pattern.
Listen, what he wore:

A dragon lying hym be-syde,
His mouth grennyng fułł wyde,
Ałł ffyghtyng as they were;
The creste, that on his hede shold stond,
Hit was ałł gold shynand,
Thus previd he hym there.

Lordys assembelid in sale,
Wełł mo than I haue in tale,
Or ellis gret wonder were.
There herd he tełł ffor certan,
That Desonełł wed shold be than,
That was hym selfe ffułł dere.
And whan he herd of that ffare,
Wors tydingis than were thare,
Might he none gladly here . . . .

He wold not in passe,
Tiłł at the myd mete was
The kyng and meny a knyght;
As they satt at theyre mete glade,
In at the hałł dur he rade
In armes ffeyre and bryght,
With a squier, that is ffre;
Vp to the lady ryduth he,
That rychely was i-dight.
'Lordys,' he said, 'among you ałł
I chalenge thre coursus in the hałł,
Or Delyuer her me with right!'

The kyng of Aragon sett her bye,
And he defendid her nobely:
'I wyłł none delyuer the.'
His son said: 'So muste I thryve,
There shałł no man just for my wiffe;
But yf youre wyłł it be,

A dragon lying beside him,
His mouth grinning wide,
All fighting as they were;
The crest, that on his head should stand,
It was all of shining gold,
Thus he was provisioned there.

Lords assembled in the hall,
Well more than I can tally,
Or else great wonder.
There he heard tell for certain,
That Desonell should be wed then,
That was to himself dear.
And when he heard of that fare,
Worse tidings than were there,
Might he none gladly hear. . . .

Torrent rides to Aragon and approaches the king and his knights at table. He demands three jousts with the prince to reclaim Desonell. The prince acknowledges he did no significant deed to win her in the first place, so he accepts Torrent's challenge.

He would not pass in
Till at lunch was
The king and many a knight;
As they sat at their meat glad,
In at the hall door he rode
In arms fiery and bright,
With a squire, that is free;
Up to the lady he rode,
That was richly adorned.
"Lords," he said, "among you all
I challenge three courses in the hall,
Before you deliver her to me with right!"

The king of Aragon set her by,
And he defended her nobly,
"I will deliver you nothing."
His son said, "So must I thrive,
There shall no man joust for my wife;
But if it be your will,

For her love did I never no dede,
I shałł to day, so god me spede:
Be-hold and ye shałł se.'
'Alas!' said Desonełł the dere,
'Fułł longe may I sitt here,
Or Torrent chalenge me.'

Trumpettes blew in the prese,
Lordys stond on the grese,
Ladyes lay ouer and be-held.
The prynce and Torrent then
Eyther to other gan ren,
Smertely in that ffeld;
Torrent sett on hym so sore,
That hors and man down he bore,
And ałł to-sheverd his sheld.
So they tombelid ałł in ffere,
That afterward of VII yere
The prynce none armes myght weld.

Torrent said: 'So god me saue,
Other two coursus wyłł I haue,
Yf ye do me law of lond.'
Gret lordys stond styłł,
They said nether good ne yłł
For tynding of his hond.
The prynce of Aragon in they barr
With litułł worshipp and sydes sare,
He had no fote on ffor to stond.
Thus thes lordys justid aye;
Better they had to haue be away,
Suche comffort there he ffond.

He wold not in passe,
Tiłł they at myd mete was,
On the other day at none.

For her love I have done no deed,
I shall today, so God help me.
Behold and you shall see."
"Alas!" Desonell said, the dear
"Long may I sit here,
Before Torrent challenges me."

Trumpets blew in the assembly,
Lords stood on the grass,
Ladies lay over and beheld.
The prince and Torrent then
Either to the other ran,
Smartly in that field;
Torrent set on him so fiercely,
That he bore down horse and man,
And shattered his shield.
So they tumbled altogether,
That afterward for seven years
The prince might not wield arms.

The joust begins. Torrent soundly beats the prince, gravely injuring, but not killing him. at their first engagement. The prince is forced to withdraw while Torrent demands his second and third jousts as is the law of the land.

Torrent said, "So God help me,
Two other courses I will have,
If you do me the law of the land."
Great lords stood still,
They said neither good nor ill
For beating of his hand.
They bore in the prince of Aragon
With little worship and sides sore,
He had no foot to stand on.
Thus these lords judged again;
Better they had to have been away,
Such comfort there they found.

He would not pass in
Till they were at lunch,
On the other day at noon.

His squiers habite he had,
Whan he to the deyse yad,
With oute couped shone,
And the hede on the bord he laid:
'Lo, sir kyng, hold this,' he said,
'Or ellis wroth we anon!'
They sett stiłł at the bord,
None of hem spake one word,
But ryght that he had done.

Torrent at the syde bord stode:
'Lystonyth, lordynges, gentiłł of blood,
For the love of god ałł-myght:
The kyng heyght me his doughter dere,
To ffyght with a ffendys ffere,
That wekyd was and wight,
To wed her to my wyffe,
And halffe his kyngdome be his liffe,
And after his days ałł his ryght.
Lokyth, lordys, you among,
Whether he do me ryght or wrong!'
Tho waried hym both kyng & knyght.

Tho said the kyng of Aragon, i-wys:
'Torrent, I wiste no thing of thys,
A gret maister arte thou!'
The kyng sware be seynt Gryffen:
'With a sword thou shalte her wynne,
Or thou haue her nowe:
For why, my son to her was wed,
Gret lordys to churche her led,
I take wittnes of ałł you.'
'Kyng Calamond, haue good day,
Thou shalt i-bye it, and I may,
To god I make avowe.'

His squires habit he had,
When he went to the dais,
Without slashed shoes,
And the head on the board he laid,
"Lo, sir king, hold this," he said,
"Or else anger we at once!"
They sat still at the table,
None of them spoke one word,
But right that he had done.

The next day Torrent again approaches the king of Aragon. He tells him in front of all his knights that the king of Portugal had already promised him Desonell in exchange for killing a giant.

Torrent stood at the side table,
"Listen, lords, of gentle blood,
For the love of God almighty.
The king called for his daughter dear,
To fight with a fiend's company,
That was wicked and white,
To her as my wife,
And half his kingdom by his life,
And after his days all his right.
Look, lords, among you,
Where he has done me right or wrong!"
Then cursed him both king and knight.

Then the king of Aragon said, I know,
"Torrent, I know nothing of this,
A great master you are!"
The king swore by Saint Griffin[14],
"With a sword you shall win her,
Before you have her now.
Because my son was to wed her,
Great lords led her to church,
I take witness of you all."
"King Calamond, have a good day,
You shall buy it, and I may,
To God make a vow."

The king of Aragon admits he was ignorant of the king of Portugal's deception and swears to take action against him in retribution.

The Emperoure of Rome ther was,
Be-twene thes kynges gan he passe
And said: 'Lordys, as sone,
This squier, that hath brought this hede,
The kyng had wend he had be dede,
And a-venturly gan he gone:
I rede you take a day of ryghtes,
And do it vppon two knyghtes,
And let no man be slon!'
Gret lordys, that were thare,
This talis lovid at that fare
And ordenyd that anon.

To the kyng the thoght com was,
To send vnto Sathanas
For a geaunt, that hight Cate,
For to make hym knyght to his hond
And sease hym in all his lond;
The messingere toke the gate.
Gret othes he sware hym than,
That he shold ffyght but with one man,
And purvey hym he bad
Iryn stavis two or thre,
For to ffyght with Torent ffre,
Though he there of ne watt.

Than take counsell kyng and knyght,
On lond that he shold not ffyght,
But ffar oute in the see,
In an yle long and brad;
A gret payn there was made,
That holdyn shold it be.
Yf Cate slow Torent, that ffre ys,
Halfe Portyngale shold be his,
To spend with dedys ffre;
And yf sir Torrent myght hym ouer-com,

The emperor of Rome was there,
He passed between the kings
And said, "Lords, as soon as,
This squire, that had brought this head,
Had gone the king turned,
And dangerously did he go.
I advise you take a day of rights,
And do it upon two knights,
And let no man be slain!"
Great lords, that were there,
Loved this tale at that fare
And ordained that at once.

The emperor of Rome mediates the dispute. He suggests Torrent do battle with one of Aragon's knights to settle the matter.

The king of Aragon decides to knight a giant named Cate. He sends a messenger to the giant informing him if he defeats Torrent he will win half the land of Portugal. He tells Torrent if he wins, he will be given half the land of Aragon.

A thought came to the king
Sent by Satan
For a giant, called Cate,
To make him a knight of his hand
And seize all of his land;
The messenger then went.
He swore great oaths then,
That he should fight but with one man,
And bade he prepare
Two or three iron staves,
To fight with Torrent free,
Though he knew nothing.

The king and knights took council,
On land that they should not fight,
But far out in the sea,
On an island long and broad;
A great effort was made,
That it should be held there.
If Cate killed Torrent, that is free,
Half of Portugal should be his,
To spend with free deeds;
And if Sir Torrent might overcome him,

He shold haue halfe Aragon,
Was better than suche thre.

The Gyaunt shipped in a while
And sett hym oute in an yle,
That was grow both grene and gay.
Sir Torrent com prekand on a stede,
Richely armed in his wede;
'Lordyngys,' gan he say,
'It is semely ffor a knyght,
Vppon a stede ffor to ffyght.'
They said sone: 'Nay,
He is so hevy, he can not ryde.
Torrent said: 'Eviłł mut he be-tyde,
Falshode, woo worth it aye!'

'Sir, takyth housełł and shrefte!'
To god he did his hondys lifte,
And thankid hym of his sond:
'Iesu Cryste, I the praye,
Send me myght and strengith this day
A-yen the ffend to stond!'
To the shipp sir Torent went,
With the grace, god had hym sent,
That was never ffayland;
Ałł the lordys of that contre,
Frome Rome vnto the Grekys se,
Stode and be-held on lond.

Whan sir Torrent in to the Ile was brought,
The shipmen lenger wold tary nought,
But hied hem sone ageyn;
The Giaunt said: 'So must I the,
Sir, thou art welcom to me,
Thy deth is not to layn!'
The ffirste stroke to hym he yaue,

He should have half of Aragon,
Was better than such three.

The giant set sail in a while
And set out to the island,
That was grown both green and gay.
Sir Torrent came riding on a steed,
Richly armed in his garments;
"Lords," he said,
"It is seemly for a knight,
To fight upon a steed."
They said soon, "No,
He is so heavy, he cannot ride."
Torrent said, "Evil he may be,
Falsehood, is worth woe always!"

An island is selected as the place of battle. Torrent and the giant both arrive by ship, but the giant is too large to ride a horse, which Torrent views as dishonorable.

"Sir, take housel and shrift!"
He lifted his hands to God,
And thanked his providence,
"Jesus Christ, I pray you,
Send me might and strength this day
Against this fiend!"
To the ship Sir Torrent went,
With the grace God had sent him,
That was never failing;
All the lords of that country,
From Rome to the Greek sea,
Stood and beheld on land.

When Sir Torrent was brought to the island,
The sailors would no longer tarry,
But left soon again;
The giant said, "So must I,
Sir, you are welcome to me,
Your death is not a secret!"
He gave the first stroke to him,

Oute of his hand flew his staff:
That thefe was fułł fayn.
Tho sir Torent went nere Cate, ...
He thought, he wold hym haue slayn.

The theff couth no better wonne,
In to the see rennyth he sone,
As faste as he myght ffare.
Sir Torrent gaderid cobed stonys,
Good and handsom ffor the nonys,
That good and round ware;
Meny of them to hym he caste,
He threw stonys on hym so faste,
That he was sad and sare.
To the ground he did hym fełł,
Men myght here the fend yełł
Halfe a myle and mare.

Sir Torent said, as he was wonne,
He thankid Iesu, Maryes son,
That kyng, that sent hym myȝt;
He said: 'Lordys, for charite,
A bote that ye send to me,
It is nere hand nyght!'
They Reysed a gale with a sayłł,
The Geaunt to lond for to trayłł,
Ałł men wonderid on that wight.
Whan that they had so done,
They went to sir Torent fułł sone
And shipped that comly knyght.

The emperoure of Rome was there,
The kynges of Pervens and of Calabere yare,
And other two or thre.
They yaue sir Torent, that he wan,
Both the Erth and the woman,

Out of his hand flew his staff.
That wretch was glad.
Then Sir Torrent went near Cate, ...
He thought, he would kill him.

The scoundrel knew no better when
Into he sea he soon ran,
As fast as he might fare.
Sir Torrent gathered cobblestones,
Good and handsome for the purpose,
That were good and round;
Many of them he cast,
He threw stones on him so fast,
That he was sad and sore.
To the ground he fell,
Men might hear the fiend yell
Half a mile and more.

> The fight begins and Torrent quickly dispatches Cate, forcing him back into the water and stoning him to death.
>
> A ship is rigged to haul the body back to the mainland, where Torrent is awarded half the lands of Aragon, the city of Cargon, and Desonell as agreed upon.

Sir Torrent said, as he knew,
He thanked Jesus, Mary's son,
That king, that sent him might;
He said, "Lords, for charity,
A boat that you sent to me,
It is near at hand!"
They traveled in a galley with a sail,
Trailing the giant to land,
All men wondered on that creature.
When thy had done so,
They went to Sir Torrent soon
And carried that comely knight.

The emperor of Rome was there,
The kings of Provence and of Calabria too,
And another two or three.
They gave Sir Torrent, that he won,
Both the earth and the woman,

And said, wełł worthy was he.
Sir Torent had in Aragon
The riche Cite of Cargon
And ałł that riche contre;
Archbeshoppes, as the law fełł,
Departid the prynce and Dissonełł
With gret solempnite.

For sir Torent the fend did fałł,
Gret lordys honoured hym ałł
And for a doughty knyght hym tase;
The kyng said: 'I vnderstond,
Thou hast fought ffor my doughter & my lond,
And wełł wonne her thou hase.'
He gaue to saint Nycholas de Barr
A grett Erldome and a simarr
That abbey of hym tas
For Iesus love, moch of myght,
That hym helpith day & nyght,
Whan he to the battełł gas.

Lordys than at the laste,
Echone on theyre way paste,
And euery man to his.
The quene of Portingale was ffayn,
That sir Torent was com agayn
And thankyd god of this.
Than said the kyng: 'I vnderstond,
Thou hast fought for my doughter & my lond,
And art my ward, i-wys,
And I wyłł not ageyn the say;
But abyde halfe yere and a day,
And broke her wełł with blis!'

Torent said: 'So muste I the,
Sith it wyłł no better be,

And said, he was well worthy.
Sir Torrent had in Aragon
The rich city of Cargon[15]
And all that rich country;
Archbishops, as the law fell,
Separated the prince and Desonell
With great solemnity.

Before Sir Torrent the fiend fell,
Great lords all honored him
And took him for a brave knight;
The king said, "I understand,
You have fought for my daughter and my land,
And you have well won her."
He gave as Saint Nicholas of Bari[16]
A great earldom and some more
He built an abbey
For Jesus' love, much of might,
That helped him day and night,
When he went to battle.

Torrent and Desonell return to Portugal. The king concedes Torrent has rightfully one her. He asks Torrent to remain in Portugal for six months and a day with her.

Then at last the lords,
Each passed on their way,
And every man to his.
The queen of Portugal was glad,
That Sir Torrent came again
And thanked God for this
Then the king said, "I understand,
That you have fought for my daughter and my land,
And are my ward, I know,
And I will not speak against you;
But abide half a year and a day,
And enjoy her well with bliss!"

Torrent said, "So I must,
After it will no better be,

I cord with that assent!'
After mete, as I you tełł,
To speke with mayden Desonełł,
To her chamber he went.
The damysełł so moche of pride
Set hym on her bed-syde,
And said: 'Welcom, verament!'
Such gestenyng he a-right,
That there he dwellid ałł nyȝt
With that lady gent.

Sir Torent dwellid thare
Twelffe wekys and mare,
Tiłł letters com hym tiłł
Fro the kyng of Norway;
For Iesus love he did hym praye,
Yf it were his wyłł,
He shold com as a doughty knyght,
With a Geaunt for to ffyght,
That wyłł his londys spyłł;
He wold hym yeve his doughter dere
And halfe Norway ffar and nere,
Both be hold and be hyłł.

Sir Torent said: 'So god me saue,
I-nough to lyve vppon I haue,
I wyłł desire no more;
But it be, for Iesu is sake
A poynt of armes for to take,
That hath helpid me be-ffore.
I yeve the here oute of my hond
To thy doughter ałł my lond,
Yf that I end thore.'
And whan he toke his way to passe,
Mo than ffyfty with hym was,
That fals to hym wore.

I accord with that assent!"
After the meeting, as I tell you,
To speak with the maiden Desonell,
To her chamber he went.
The damsel of so much pride
Set him on her bedside,
And said, "Welcome, truly!"
She displayed such hospitality,
That he dwelled there all night
With that gentle lady.

Three months later a message arrives from the king of Norway requesting Torrent come to his land to fight a giant. Torrent, despite having Desonell, wealth, and land decides to go anyway, for the honor of it.

Sir Torrent dwelled there
Twelve weeks and more,
Till letters came to him
From the king of Norway;
For Jesus' love he prayed,
If it were his will,
He should come as a brave knight,
To fight with a giant,
That destroyed his land;
He would give him his dear daughter
And half of Norway far and near,
Both by hold and by hill.

Sir Torrent said, "So God help me,
I have enough to live upon,
I will desire no more;
But it be, for Jesus' sake
A task of arms to take,
That has helped me before.
I give you here out of my hand
To your daughter all my land,
If that I die there."
And when he took his way to pass,
More than fifty were with him,
That were false to him.

Syr Torent to the lady went,
Fułł curtesly and gent: . . . .
'Desonełł, haue good day!
I muste now on my jurnay,
A kyngis lond for to fend.
Thes gold rynges I shałł yeve the,
Kepe them wełł, my lady ffre,
Yf god a child vs send!'
She toke the ryngis with moche care,
Thries in sownyng fełł she thare,
Whan she saw, that he wold wend.

Shipp and takyłł they dight,
Stede and armour ffor to ffyght
To the bote they bare.
Gentilmen, that were hend,
Toke her leve at theyre frend,
With hym ffor to fare.
Kyng Colomond, is not to layn,
He wold, that he cam nevure agayn;
There fore god yeff hym care!
So within the ffyfty dayes
He Come in to the lond of Norways,
Hard Contre ffound he thare.

Thus sir Torrent, for soth, is fare,
A noble wynd droffe hym thare,
Was blowyng oute of the weste.
Of the Coste of Norway they had a sight . . . .
Of sayling they were ałł preste.
So ffeyre a wynd had the knyght,
A litułł be-ffore the mydnyght
He Rode be a foreste.
The shipmen said: 'We be shent;
Here dwellith a geaunt, verament,
On his lond are we kest!'

Torrent makes ready to depart. The king of Portugal supplies him with fifty men as companions.

Before leaving Torrent gives Desonell two gold rings to give to their children should she bear any in his absence.

Sir Torrent went to his lady,
Courteously and gently, ...
"Desonell, have a good day!
I must now journey,
To a king's land for a fiend.
These gold rings I shall give you,
Keep them well, my lady free,
If God sends us a child!"
She took the rings with much grief,
She fell swooning thrice there,
When she saw that he would go.

They prepared ship and tackle,
Steed and armor for the fight
They bore to the boat.
Gentlemen, that were noble,
Took their leave at their friend,
To fare with him.
King Calamond, did not doubt,
He would never come again;
Therefore God gave him grief!
So within the fifty days
He came into the land of Norway,
Hard country he found there.

Thus Sir Torrent, for truth his journey,
A noble wind drove him there,
Was blowing out of the west.
Of the coast of Norway they had sight . . . .
Of sailing they were all rushed.
So fair a wind the knight had,
A little before midnight
He rode by a forest.
The sailors said, "We are ruined;
Here dwells a giant, truly,
On his land we are cast!"

The maistershipmon said: 'Nowe
I Rede, we take down sayle & Rowe,
While we haue this tyde.
Sir,' he said, 'be god ałlmyght,
The giant lieth euery nyght
On the mowntayn here be-syde;
My lord the kyng wyłł not ffyght,
Tiłł he of you haue a sight,
On you ys ałł his pryde!'
Sir Torrent said: 'Here my hond!
Sith we be ryven on this lond,
To nyght wyłł I ryde.'

Sir Torent armyd hym anon
And his knyghtes euerychone
With sheld and spere in hond.
The shipmen said: 'As mut I thryve,
I Rede, that euery man other shryve,
Or that we go to the lond.'
Sir Torent said: 'As god me spede,
We wiłł firste se that ffede,
My lord was never failand!
Gentilmen, make chere good,
For Iesu love, that died on Rood,
He wiłł be oure waraunt!'

In a forest can they passe,
Of Brasiłł, saith the boke, it was,
With bowes brod and wyde.
Lyons and berys there they ffand
And wyld bestes aboute goand,
Reysing on euery side.
Thes men of armes, with trayn
To the shipp they flew agayn
In to the see at that tyde;
Fast from land row they be-gan,

The master sailor said, "Now
I advise, we take down sail and row,
While we have this tide.
Sir," he said, "by God almighty,
The giant lies every night
On the mountain here beside;
My lord the king will not fight,
Till he has sight of you,
On you is all his pride!"
Sir Torrent said, "Hear my pledge!
After we arrive on this land,
Tonight I will ride."

After sailing for fifty days, Torrent and his men arrive in the waters off Norway.

The men are terrified of that strange land, but Torrent assures them all will be well.

Sir Torrent armed himself at once
And his knights every one
With shield and spear in hand.
The sailors said, "As I may thrive,
I advise, that every man shrive the other,
Before we go to land."
Sir Torrent said, "As God help me,
We will first see that enemy,
My lord was never fleeing!
Gentlemen, make good cheer,
For Jesus' love, that died on the cross,
He will be our guardian!"

In a forest they passed,
Of Brazil[17], the book says it was,
With broad and wide boughs.
Lions and bears there they found
And wild beasts going about,
Racing on every side.
These men of arms, with treachery
To the ship they flew again
Into the sea at the tide;
Fast from land they began to row,

Despite Torrent's assurances, all fifty men desert him in the wilderness and return to their ship.

A-bove they left that gentilman,
With wyld beestis to haue kyde.

The shipmen of the same lond
Ryved vp, I vnderstond,
In another lond off hold.
To the chamber they toke the way,
There the kyng hym selfe lay,
And fals talis hym told . . . .
For he wold not the geaunt abyde,
For ałł this contrey feyre and wyde,
Thouȝ he yeff it hym wold.

'Sir kyng, ye haue youre selfe
Erlis doughty be ten or twelfe,
Better know I none:
Send youre messingeris ffar and wyde,
For to ffełł the geauntes pride,
That youre doughter hath tane.'
'I had lever to haue that knyght;
With hym is grace of god ałłmyȝt,
To be here at his bane.'
Fułł litułł wist that riche kyng
Of sir Torrent es ryding
In the forest ałł alone.

Thorouȝ helpe of god that with hym was,
Fro the wyld bestis gan he passe
To an hye hyłł.
A litułł while be-fore the day
He herd in a valey
A dynnyng and a yełł.
Theder than riduth he,
To loke, what thing it myȝt be,
What adventure thare be-fełł.
It were two dragons stiff and strong,

Above they left that gentleman.
To meet with wild beasts.

The deserters arrive in the hall of the king of Norway, who refuses to fight the giant on his own or send his own men to fight. He insists on awaiting Torrent's arrival, though he is unaware of the men's treachery and cowardice.

The sailors of the same land
Arrived, I understand,
In another land of the hold.
To the chamber they took the way,
There the king himself lay
And told him false tales . . . .
For he would not endure the giant,
For all this country fair and wide,
Though it would give him power.

"Sir king, you have yourself
Brave earls ten or twelve,
I know no better.
Send you messengers far and wide,
To fell the giant's pride,
That has taken your daughter."
"I had rather have that knight;
With him is God's almighty grace,
To be here as his bane."
Little knew that rich king
Of Sir Torrent's riding
In the forest all alone.

Through the help of God that was with him,
He passed from the wild beasts
To a high hill.

Torrent pushes on alone, eventually coming upon two fearsome dragons.

A little while before the day
He heard in a valley
A clamor and a yell.
Thither then he rode,
To look what thing it might be,
What adventure there befell.
It was two dragons stiff and strong,

Vppon theyre lay they sat and song,
Be-side a depe wełł.

Sir Torent said thanne
To god, that made man
And died vppon a tree:
'Lord, as thou mayst ałł weld,
Yeve me grace, to wyn the feld
Of thes ffendys onfre!'
Whan he had his prayers made,
Pertely to hem he Rade
And one thorouȝ oute bare he.
Thus sped the knyght at his comyng
Thorough the helpe of hevyn kyng:
Lord, lovid muste thou be!

The other dragon wold not flee, ...
But showith ałł his myght;
He smote ffire, that lothely thing,
As it were the lightnyng,
Vppon that comly knyght.
There fore sir Torent wold nto lett,
But on the dragon fast he bett
And over-come that foule wight.
Tho anon the day sprong,
Fowles Rose, mery they song,
The sonne a-Rose on hyȝt.

Torent of the day was fułł blithe,
And of the valey he did hym swith,
As fast as euer he may.
To a mowntayn he rode ryght,
Of a castełł he had a sight
With towrys hyȝe and gay . . . .
He come in to an hyȝe strete,
Few folke gan he mete,

Where they lay they sat and sang,
Beside a deep spring.

Sir Torrent said then
To God that made man
And died upon a tree,
"Lord, as you may wield all,
Give me grace to win the field
From these wicked fiends!"
When he had made his prayers,
Boldly he rode to them
And he bore one through.
Thus succeeded the knight at his coming
Through the help of heaven's king
Lord, loved must you be!

Torrent prays for strength and engages the two dragons. He kills one quickly, but the other puts up a strong fight before being defeated.

The other dragon would not flee, ...
But showed all his might;
He smote fire, that horrible thing,
As if it were lightning,
Upon that comely knight.
Therefore Sir Torrent would not delay,
But beat fast on the dragon
And overcame the foul creature.
Then at once spang the day,
Fowls rose, merrily they sang,
The sun rose on high.

Torrent was glad for the day,
And quickly left the valley
As fast as he could.
He rode to a mountain
He had sight of a castle
With towers high and gay. . . .
He came into a high street,
He met a few folk,

To wis hym the way.

To the gatys tho he Rade;
Fułł craftely they were made
Of Irun and eke of tree.
One tre stonding there he ffond:
Nyne oxen of that lond
Shold not drawe the tre.
The Giaunt wrought vp his wałł
And laid stonys gret and smałł:
A lothely man was he.
'Now,' quod Torrent, 'I not, whare,
My squiers be ffro me to fare,
Euer waried they be!

'Lord god, what is beste,
So Iesu me helpe, Est or Weste,
I Can not Rede to say.
Yf I to the shipp fare,
No shipmen ffynd I thare;
It is long, sith they were away.
Other wayes yf I wend,
Wyld bestis wyłł me shend:
Falshede, woo worth it aye!
I ffyght here, Iesu, for thy sake;
Lord, to me kepe thou take,
As thou best may!'

Down light this gentiłł knyght,
To Rest hym a litułł wight,
And vnbrydelid his stede
And let hym bayte on the ground,
And aventid hym in that stound,
There of he had gret nede.
The Gyaunt yode and gaderid stone
And sye, where the knyght gan gone,

To show him the way.

To the gates he then rode;
Skillfully they were made
Of iron and also of wood.
One tree standing there he found;
Nine oxen of that land
Should not draw the tree.
The giant wrought up his wall
And laid stones great and small.
A horrible man he was.
"Now," Torrent said, "I know why,
My squires flew from me,
Ever cursed they are!"

Torrent eventually comes to a road where some travelers point him toward a castle. There he finds the giant, prays for guidance, and takes a rest.

"Lord God, what is best,
So Jesus help me, east or west,
I cannot decide.
If I flee to the ship,
No sailor will I find there;
It is long after they were away.
Other ways if I go,
Wild beasts will destroy me.
Deceit, woe worth it always!
I fight here, Jesus, for your sake;
Lord, take and keep me,
As you best may!"

This gentle knight lay down,
To rest a little while,
And unbridled his steed
And let him graze on the ground,
And cooled himself for a time,
There he had great need.
The giant went and gathered stones
And saw, where the knight had gone,

Ałł armed in dede;
And wot ye wełł and not wene,
Whan eyther of hem had other sene,
Smertely they rerid her dede.

For that sir Torent had hym sene,
He worth vppon his stede, I wene,
And Iesu prayde he tiłł:
'Mary son, thou here my bone,
As I am in venturus stad come,
My jurnay to fułł-ffyłł!'
A voys was fro hevyn sent
And said: 'Be blith, sir Torent,
And yeve the no thing yłł,
To ffyght with my lordys enemy:
Whether that thou lyve or dye,
Thy mede the quyte he wyłł!'

Be that the giaunt had hym dight,
Cam ageyn that gentiłł knyght,
As bold as eny bore;
He bare on his nek a croke,
Woo were the man, that he ouertoke,
It was twelfe ffote and more.
'Sir,' he said, 'ffor charite,
Loke, curtes man that thou be,
Yf thy wyłł ware:
I haue so fought ałł this nyght
With thy II dragons wekyd and wight,
They haue bett me fułł sore.'

The Geaunt said: 'Be my fay,
Wors tydinges to me this day
I myght not goodly here.
Thorough the valey as thou cam,
My two dragons hast thou slan,

All armed in deed;
And know you well and don't doubt,
When either of them had seen the other,
Quickly they rose to their task.

Before Sir Torrent had seen him,
He mounted upon his steed, I know,
And prayed to Jesus,
"Mary's son, hear my prayer,
As I have come to adventure,
To fulfil my journey!"
A voice was sent from heaven
And said, "Be happy, Sir Torrent,
And give yourself no ill,
To fight with my lord's enemy,
Whether you live or die,
He will pay you your reward!"

An angelic voice comforts Torrent, assuring him that live or die he will be justly rewarded.

By the time the giant had prepared,
He came again to that gentle knight,
As bold as any boar;
He bore on his neck a crook,
Woe were the man that he overtook,
It was twelve foot and more.
"Sir," he said, "for charity,
Look, courteous man that you are,
If you will.
I have so fought all this night
With your two dragons wicked and swift,
They have beat me sorely."

The giant said, "By my faith,
Worse tidings to me this day
I might not hear.
Through the valley as you came,
My two dragons you have slain,

My solempnite they were.
To the I haue fułł good gate;
For thou slow my brother Cate,
That thou shalte by fułł dere!'
Be-twene the giaunt and the knyght
Men myght se buffettes right,
Who so had be there.

Sir Torent yaue to hym a brayd;
He levid that the aungełł said,
Of deth yaue he nought.
In to the brest he hym bare,
His spere hede lefte he thare,
So eviłł was hitt bythought.
The Giaunt hym ayen smate
Thorough his sheld and his plate,
In to the flesh it sought;
And sith he pullith at his croke,
So fast in to the flesh it toke,
That oute myʒt he gete it nought.

On hym he hath it broke,
Glad pluckys there he toke,
Set sadly and sare.
Sir Torent stalworth satt,
Oute of his handys he it gatt,
No lenger dwellid he thare.
In to the water he cast his sheld,
Croke and ałł to-geders it held,
Fare after, how so euer it ffare.
The Geaunt folowid with ałł his mayn,
And he come never quyk agayn:
God wold, that so it ware.

Sir Torent bet hym there,
Tiłł that this fend did were,

My joy they were.
To [kill] you have full reason;
For you slew my brother Cate,
You shall pay dearly!"
Between the giant and the knight
Men might see blows,
Whoso had been there.

The giant approaches Torrent. Torrent tells him he has just killed to dragons. The giant says those were his pets and that Cate, the giant Torrent killed most recently, was his brother.

Sir Torrent gave him a reproach;
He believed what the angel said,
Of death he cared not.
Into the breast he bore him,
He left his spear head there,
So evil was his thought.
He smote the giant again
Through his shield and his plate,
Into the flesh it sought;
And after he pulled at his crook,
So fast in to the flesh it took,
That he might not get it out.

A terrible fight ensues. The giant, armed with a huge crook, buries it in Torrent's shield, greatly injuring him. Torrent pries the shield and crook from his wound and casts it into a nearby lake. The giant dives in to recover his weapon but is drowned.

He broke it on him,
Glad pulls he took there,
Sat sadly and sore.
Sir Torrent sat stalwart,
Out of his hands he dropped it,
He no longer stayed there.
Into the water he cast his shield,
Crook and all together it held,
Thereafter howsoever it fared.
The giant followed with all his strength,
And he came never quick again.
God willed that it were so.

Sir Torrent beat him there,
Till that fiend were dead,

Or he thens wend.
On hym had he hurt but ane,
Lesse myght be a mannus bane,
But god is fułł hend:
Thorough grace of hym, that ałł shałł weld,
There the knyght had the feld,
Such grace god did hym send.
Be than it nyed nere hand nyȝt,
To a castełł he Rode right,
Ałł nyght there to lend.

In the castełł found he nought,
That god on the Rode bought;
High vppon a toure,
As he caste a side lokyng,
He saw a lady in her bed syttyng,
White as lylye ffloure;
Vp a-Rose that lady bryght,
And said: 'Welcom, sir knyght,
That fast art in stoure!'
'Damysełł, welcom mut thou be!
Graunt thou me, for charite,
Of one nyghtis soioure!'

'By Mary,' said that lady clere,
'Me for-thinkith, that thou com here,
Thy deth now is dight;
For here dwellith a geaunt,
He is clepud Weraunt,
He is to the deviłł be-taught.
To day at morn he toke his croke,
Forth at the yates the way he toke,
And said, he wold haue a draught;
And here be chambers two or thre,
In one of hem I shałł hide the,
God the saue ffrome harmes right!'

Before he went thence.
He had but one injury on him,
Less might be a man's bane,
But God is kind.
Through his grace, that shall wield all,
There the knight had the field,
Such grace God sent him.
By then night was near at hand,
To a castle he rode,
To stay there all night.

Torrent rides from the field to the castle where he finds a lady imprisoned there awaiting the giant's return. She offers to hide Torrent.

In the castle he found no one,
That God on the cross bought;
High upon a tower,
As he cast a look aside,
He saw a lady sitting in her bed,
White as a lily flower;
Up rose that lady bright,
And said, "Welcome, sir knight,
That is strong in battle!"
"Damsel, welcome might you be!
Grant me, for charity,
One night's succor!"

"By Mary," said that fair lady,
"I think that since you've come here,
Your death is now prepared;
For here dwells a giant,
He is called Weraunt,
He is taught by the devil.
This morning he took his crook,
Forth at the gates the way he took,
And said he would have a walk;
And here by chambers two or three,
In one of them I shall hide you,
God save you from harm!"

'Certayn,' tho said the knyght,
'That theffe I saw to nyght,
Here be-side a slade.
He was a ferly freke in ffyght,
With hym faught a yong knyght,
Ech on other laid good lade;
Me thought wełł, as he stode,
He was of the fendus blood,
So Rude was he made.
Dame, yf thou leve not me,
Com nere, and thou shalt se,
Which of hem abade.'

Blith was that lady bryght
For to se that selly sight:
With the knyght went she.
Whan she cam, where the Geaunt lay,
'Sir,' she said, 'parmaffay
I wott wełł, it is he.
Other he was of god ałł-myght
Or seynt George, oure lady kny3t,
That there his bane hath be.
Yf eny cryston man smyte hym down,
He is worthy to haue renown
Thorough oute ałł crystiaunte.'

'I haue wonder,' said the knyght,
'How he gate the, lady bryght,
Fro my lord the kyng.'
'Sir,' she said, 'verament,
As my fader on huntyng went
Erly in a mornyng,
Fore his men pursued a dere,
To his castełł, that stondith here,
That doth my hondys wryng,
This Giaunt hym toke, wo he be!

"Certainly," then the knight said,
"That wretch I saw tonight,
Here beside a valley.
He was a terrible warrior in a fight,
A young knight fought with him,
Each on the other laid a good blow;
I thought well, as he stood,
He was of the fiend's blood,
So rudely was he made.
Dame, if you don't believe me,
Come near, and you shall see,
Which of them lives."

Torrent assures the lady the giant is dead and takes her to his body to see for herself.

She tells Torrent she is the king's daughter and that the giant imprisoned him one day and would only release him in exchange for her.

Happy was that lady bright
To see that wondrous sight.
She went with the knight.
When she came, where the giant lay,
"Sir," she said, "by my faith
I know well, it is he.
Else he was God almighty
Or Saint George[18], our lady knight,
That there his death has been.
If any Christian man smote him down,
He is worthy to have renown
Throughout all Christianity."

"I wonder," the knight said,
"How he got you, fair lady,
From my lord the king."
"Sir," she said, "truly,
As my father went hunting
Early in the morning,
Before his men he pursued a dear,
To this castle, that stands here,
That does wring my hands,
This giant took him, woe to him!

For his love he gevith hym me,
He wold none other thinge.'

Forth she brought bred and wyne,
Fayn he was for to dyne . . . .
This knyght made noble chere,
Though that he woundid were
With the Geaunt strong.

Sir Torrent dwellid no lenger thare,
Than he myȝt away fare
With that lady bryght.
'Now, Iesu, that made hełł,
Send me on lyve to Desonełł,
That I my trouth to plight!'
Tho sye they be a forest syde
Men of armes ffaste ride
On coursers comly dight.
The lady said: 'So mvst I thee,
It is my fader, is com for me,
With the Geaunt to ffyght.'

An harood said anon right:
'Yon I se an armed knyght,
And no squier, but hym one:
He is so big of bone & blood,
He is the Geaunt, be the Rode!'
Som seith, he riduth vppon.
'Nay,' said the kyng, 'verament,
It is the knyght, that I after sent,
I thanke god and seynt Iohn,
For the Geaunt slayn hath he
And wonne my doughter, weł is me!
Ałł his men are atone!'

Wott ye weł, with Ioy and blis

For his love he gave me to him,
He would have no other thing."

She brought forth bread and wine,
Glad he was to dine. . . .
This knight made noble cheer,
Though he was wounded
By the strong giant.

Sir Torrent dwelled there no longer,
Then he might travel away
With that lady bright.
"Now Jesus, that made hell,
Send me alive to Desonell,
That I may marry her!"
Then by a forest side
Men of arms fast rode
On horses well adorned.
The lady said, "So I must,
It is my father come for me,
To fight with the giant."

Torrent remains with the lady in the castle but a short time before the two ride out. They are soon met by a group of knights and escorted back to the king's hall.

A herald said at once,
"Yonder I see an armored knight,
And no squire, but him alone.
He is so big of bone and blood,
He is the giant by the cross!"
Some say, he rides.
"No," said the king, "Truly,
It is the knight that I sent after,
I thank God and Saint John,
For he had slain the giant
And won my daughter!
All his men are taken!"

Know you well, with joy and bliss

Sir Torent there recevid ys,
As doughty man of dede.
The kyng and other lordys gent
Said, 'Welcom, sir Torent,
In to this vncouth thede!'
In to a state they hym brought,
Lechis sone his woundis sought;
They said, so god hem spede,
Were there no lyve but ane,
His liffe they wyłł not vndertane,
For no gold ne ffor mede.

The lady wist not or than,
That he was hurt, that gentilman,
And sith she went hym tyłł;
She sought his woundus and said thare:
'Thou shalte lyve and welfare,
Yf the no-thing evyłł!
My lord the kyng hath me hight,
That thou shalt wed me, sir knyght,
The fforward ye to fulle ffyłł.'
'Damysełł, loo here my hond:
And I take eny wyffe in this lond,
It shałł be at thy wyłł!'

Gendres was that ladyes name.
The Geauntes hede he brought hame,
And the dragons he brought.
Mene myght here a myle aboute,
How on the dede hedys they did shoute,
For the shame, that they hem wrought,
Both with dede and with tong
Fyfte on the hedys dong,
That to the ground they sought.
Sir Torrent dwellid thare
Twelfe monythis and mare,

Sir Torrent was received there,
As a man of brave deeds.
The king and other noble lords
Said, "Welcome, Sir Torrent,
Into this unknown land!"
Into an estate they brought him,
Leeches soon sought his wounds;
They said, so God give him fortune,
Were there no lives but one,
His life they would not take,
For neither gold nor for reward.

It's only now that the lady, Gendres, realizes Torrent had been wounded and needed care. He is given treatment and is informed the king will wed her to him as a reward for his deeds. Torrent politely refuses.

The lady knew not before then,
That he was hurt, that gentleman,
And after she went to him;
She sought his wounds and said there,
"You shall live and fare well,
If nothing evil!
My lord the king has told me,
That you shall wed me, sir knight,
A promise you will fulfill."
"Damsel, look here in my hand.
If I take any wife in this land,
It shall be at your will!"

The treachery of Torrent's fifty companions is brought to light. They are beaten and chased back to their boat and cast out to sea. All but one perish on the voyage back to Portugal.

Torrent will remain in Norway for a year.

Gendres was that lady's name.
The giant's head he brought home,
And the dragons he brought.
Men might hear a mile about,
How on the dead heads they did shout,
For the shame, that they wrought,
Both with deed and with tongue
Beat the fifty on the heads,
That to the ground they sought.
Sir Torrent dwelled there
Twelve months and more,

That ffurther my3t he nought.

The kyng of Norway said: 'Nowe,
Fals thevis, woo worth you,
Ferly soteł were ye:
Ye said, the knyght wold not com:
Swith oute of my kyngdome,
Or hangid shał ye be!'
His squiers, that fro hym fled,
With sore strokys are they spred
Vppon the wanne see,
And there they drenchid euery man,
Saue one knave, that to lond cam,
And woo be-gone is he.

The child, to lond that god sent,
In Portyngale he is lent,
In a riche town,
That hath hight be her day,
And euer shał, as I you say,
The town of Peron.
By-fore the kyng he hym sett,
'Fuł weł thy men, lord, the grett,
And in the see did they drown.'
Desoneł said: 'Where is Torent?'
'In Norway, lady, verament.'
On sownyng feł she down.

As she sownyd, this lady myld,
Men my3t se tokenyng of her child,
Steryng on her right syde.
Gret Ruth it was to teł,
How her maydens on her feł,
Her to Couer and to hide.
Tho the kyng said: 'My doughter, do way!
By god, thy myrth is gone for aye,

Then further might he not.

The king of Norway said, "Now,
False wretches, woe unto you,
Terribly cunning you were.
You said the knight would not come.
Get out of my kingdom swiftly,
Or you will be hanged!"
His squires that had fled from him,
With sore strokes they scattered
Upon the dark sea,
And there they drowned every man,
Save one knave, that came to land,
And woebegone is he.

The child, that God sent to land,
Landed in Portugal,
In a rich town,
That was high in her day,
And ever shall, as I say to you,
To town of Peron.
Before the king he sat himself,
"Full well your men, lord, the great,
And in the sea they drowned."
Desonell said, "Where is Torrent?"
"In Norway, lady, truly."
She fell down swooning.

As she swooned, this mild lady,
Men might see signs of her child,
Stirring on her right side.
Great pity it was to tell,
How her maidens fell on her,
To cover and hide her.
Then the king said, "My daughter, go away!
By God, your mirth is gone forever,

> The lone survivor reaches Portugal and informs the king and Desonell that Torrent remained in Norway. Desonell faints and it is then that everyone sees she is pregnant.
>
> The king, infuriated that Desonell is with child despite never having wed Torrent, says he will cast her and the child out to sea as punishment.

Spousage wyłł thou none bide!
There fore thou shalt in to the see
And that Bastard with-in the,
To lerne you ffor to ride.'

Erlis and Barons, that were good,
By-fore the kyng knelid and stode
For that lady free.
The quene, her moder, on knees fełł,
'For Iesu is love, that harood hełł,
Lord, haue mercy on me!
That ylke dede, that she hath done,
It was with an Erlis sonne,
Riche man i-nough is he;
And yf ye wyłł not let her lyve,
Right of lond ye her yeve,
Tiłł she delyuerd be!'

Thus the lady dwellith there,
Tyll that she delyuerd were
Of men children two;
In all poyntes they were gent,
And like they were to sir Torent;
For his love they sufferid woo.
The kyng said: 'So mut I thee,
Thou shalte in-to the see
With oute wordys moo.
Euery kyngis doughter ffer and nere,
At the shałł they lere,
Ayen the law to do.'

Gret ruth it was to se,
Whan they led that lady ffree
Oute of her faders lond.
The quene wexid tho nere wood
For her doughter, that gentiłł ffode,

You will not be married!
Therefore you shall go into the sea
And that bastard with you,
To teach you to ride[19]."

Earls and barons that were good
Knelt before the king and stood
For that lady free.
The queen, her mother, fell on her knees,
"For Jesus' love, that harrowed hell,
Lord, have mercy on me!
That same deed that she has done,
It was with an earl's son,
He is a rich enough man;
And if you will not let her live,
It's the law of the land she live,
Till she delivers!"

The queen intervenes and says the law commands the king wait until the child is born before banishing Desonell.

Desonell eventually gives birth to twins.

Thus the lady dwelled there,
Till she delivered
Two boy children;
In all aspects they were noble,
And like they were to Sir Torrent;
For his love they suffered woe.
The king said, "So must I,
You shall go into the sea
Without more words.
Every king's daughter far and near,
They will learn from you,
What is against the law to do."

Great pity it was to see,
When they led that lady free
Out of her father's land.
The queen grew nearly mad
For her daughter, that gentle child,

And knyghtis stode wepand;
A cloth of silke gan they ta
And partyd it be-twene hem twa,
Therin they were wonde.
Whan they had shypped that lady ying,
An hunderid fełł in sownyng
At Peron on the sond.

Whan that lady was downe fall,
On Iesu Cryste dyd she call;
Down knelid that lady clene:
'Rightfull god, ye me sende
Iesu Cryste, that com vp here
On this strond, as I wenyd
Some good londe, on to lende,
That my chyldren may crystonyd bene!'
She said, 'Knyghtis and ladyes gent,
Grete wełł my lord, sir Torrent,
Yeff ye hym euer sene!'
The wynd Rose ayen the nyght,
Fro lond it blew that lady bryght
Vppon the see so grene.

Wyndes and weders haue her drevyn,
Þat in a forest she is revyn,
There wyld beestis were;
The see was eb, and went her ffroo,
And lefte her and her children two
Alone with-oute ffere.
Her one child woke and be-gan to wepe,
The lady a-woke oute of her slepe
And said: 'Be stiłł, my dere,
Iesu Cryst hath sent vs lond;
Yf there be any cryston man nere hond,
We shałł haue som socoure here.'

And knights stood weeping;
A cloth of silk they took
And parted it in two between them,
Therein they were parted.
When they had shipped that young lady,
A hundred fell in swooning
At Peron on the sand.

The queen and her daughter split a piece of fabric between them. If they are ever reunited, they will recognize each other by their respective half.

Desonell and the children are put in a rickety boat and cast out to sea.

When that lady fell down,
She called on Jesus Christ;
That excellent lady knelt down,
"Righteous God, send me
Jesus Christ, that came up here
On this strand, as I go,
Some good land to land on,
That my children may be kindly christened!"
She said, "Knights, and noble ladies,
Greet well my lord, Sir Torrent,
If you ever see him!"
The wind rose against the night,
From land it blew that fair lady
Upon the sea so green.

Desonell's boat comes ashore in an unfamiliar land.

Winds and weather drove her,
That she arrived in a forest,
Wild beasts were there;
And the sea ebbed, and went from her,
And left her and her two children
Alone without company.
Her one child woke and began to weep,
The lady awoke out of her sleep
And said, "Be still my dear,
Jesus Christ sent us to land;
If there be any Christian man near at hand,
We shall have some succor here."

The carefułł lady was fułł blith,
Vp to lond she went swith,
As fast as euer she myght.
Tho the day be-gan to spryng,
Foules a-Rose and mery gan syng
Delicious notys on hight.
To a mowntayn went that lady ffree:
Sone was she warr of a Cite
With towrus ffeyre and bryght.
There fore, i-wys, she was fułł fayn,
She sett her down, as I herd sayn,
Her two children ffor to dight.

Vppon the low the lady ffound
An Erber wrought with mannus hond,
With herbis, that were good.
A Grype was in the mowntayn wonne,
A way he bare her yong son
Ouer a water fflood,
Over in to a wyldernes,
There seynt Antony ermet wes,
There as his chapełł stode.
The other child down gan she ly,
And on the ffoule did shoute & crye,
That she was nere hond wood.

Vp she rose ageyn the rough,
With sorofułł hert and care Inough,
Carefułł of blood and bone . . . .
She sye, it myght no better be,
She knelid down vppon her kne,
And thankid god and seynt Iohn.

There come a libard vppon his pray,
And her other child bare away,
She thankid god there

Desonell spies a city in the distance and sets her children down to prepare for the journey there. Suddenly a griffin swoops out of the sky and snatches up one of the children, carrying it over the sea. Shortly thereafter a leopard appears and snatches the other child away.

The sorrowful lady was glad,
She went quickly onto land,
As fast as she might ever.
The day began to spring,
Fowls arose and sang merrily
Delicious notes on high.
To a mountain went that lady free
Soon she was aware of a city
With towers fair and bright.
Therefore, I know, she was glad,
She sat down, as I heard said,
To prepare her two children.

Upon the place the lady found
An arbor wrought by men's hands,
With herbs that were good.
A griffin dwelling on the mountain,
Bore away her young son
Over a sea,
Over into a wilderness,
There Saint Anthony[20] the hermit was,
His chapel stood there.
She laid the other child down,
And on the creature she shouted and cried,
That she was nearly mad.

She rose up against the rough ground,
With sorrowful heart and enough grief,
Saddened to blood and bone. . . .
She sighed, it might not be better,
She knelt down upon her knee,
And thanked God and Saint John.

There came a leopard upon his pray,
And her other child he bore away,
She thanked God there

And his moder Mary bryght.
This lady is lefte alone ryght:
The sorow she made there . . . .

That she myght no further ffare:
'Of one poynt,' she sayd, 'is my care,
As I do now vnderstond,
So my children crystenyd were,
Though they be with beestes there,
Theyre liffe is in goddus hond.'
The kyng of Ierusalem had bene
At his brothers weddyng, I wene,
That was lord of ałł that lond.
As he com homward on his way,
He saw where the liberd lay
With a child pleyand.

Torrent had yeve her ringes two,
And euery child had one of tho,
Hym with ałł to saue.
The kyng said: 'Be Mary myld,
Yonder is a liberd with a child,
A mayden or a knave.'
Tho men of armes theder went,
Anon they had theyre hors spent,
Her guttys oute she Rave.
For no stroke wold she stynt;
Tiłł they her slew with speris dynt,
The child myght they not haue.

Vp they toke the child ying
And brought it be-ffore the kyng
And vndid the swathing band,
As his moder be-ffore had done,
A gold ryng they ffound sone,
Was closud in his hond.

And his mother Mary fair.
This lady is left alone,
With the sorrow she made there. . . .

That she might fare no further.
"Of one point," she said, "is my grief,
As I now understand,
So my children were christened,
Though they be with beasts there,
Their lives are in God's hands."
The king of Jerusalem had been
At his brother's wedding, I know,
That was lord of that land.
As he came homeward on his way,
He saw where the leopard lay
Playing with the child.

The king of Jerusalem is returning home from his brother's wedding when he and his men come upon a leopard toying with a child. The men kill the beast and rescue the child, who is found to be holding a gold ring in his hand, one of the two gifted to Desonell by Torrent.

Torrent had given her two rings,
And each child had one of them,
To keep with him.
The king said, "By Mary mild,
Yonder is a leopard with a child,
A maiden or a knave."
The men of arms thither went,
At once they had spent their horses,
She tore out their guts.
For no stroke would she stop;
Till they slew her with spear blows,
The child might they not have.

They took up the young child
And brought it before the king
And undid the swathing band,
As his mother had done beforehand.
A gold ring the soon found,
Was closed in his hand.

Tho said the kyng of Ierusalem:
'This child is come of gentilł teme,
Where euer this beest hym ffond.
The boke of Rome berith wytnes,
The kyng hym namyd Leobertus,
That was hent in hethyn lond.

Two squiers to the town gan flyng,
And a noryse to the child did bryng,
Hym to kepe ffrome greme.
He led it in to his own lond
And told the quene, how he it ffond
By a water streme.
Whan the lady saw the ryng,
She said, with-oute lettyng:
'This child is com of gentilł teme:
Thou hast none heyre, thy lond to take,
For Iesu love thou sholdist hym make
Prynce of Ierusalem.'

Now, in boke as we rede,
As seynt Antony aboute yede,
Byddyng his orysoun,
Of the gripe he had a sight,
How she flew in a fflight,
To her birdus was she boun.
Be-twene her clawes she bare a child:
He prayed to god and Mary myld,
On lyve to send it down.
That man was wełł with god ałł-myȝt,
At his fote gan she light,
That foule of gret renown.

Vp he toke the child there,
To his auter he did it bere,
There his chapełł stode.

Then the king of Jerusalem said,
"This child comes from noble stock,
Wherever this beast found him.
The book of Rome bears witness,
The king named him Leobertus,
That was taken in heathen lands.

The king sends for a nurse, and the child is brought back to Jerusalem. The queen tells the king to raise the child and make him his heir.

Two squires flew to the town,
And brought a nurse to the child,
To keep him from harm.
He led it into his own land
And told the queen how he found it
By a stream.
When the lady saw the ring,
She said without delaying,
"This child comes from worthy stock
You have no heir to take your land,
For Jesus' love you should make him
Prince of Jerusalem."

Now in the book as we read,
As Saint Anthony went about,
Saying his prayers,
He had sight of the griffin,
How she flew in flight,
To her young she was bound.
Between her claws she bore a child.
He prayed to God and Mary mild,
To send it down alive.
That man was well with God almighty,
She alit at his foot,
That fowl of great renown.

In another land, the griffin alights with a child at the foot of the hermit Saint Anthony. Anthony takes up the child and runs to his father, the king of Greece.

He took up the child there,
And bore it to his altar,
Where his chapel stood.

A knave child there he ffond,
There was closud in his hond
A gold ryng riche and good.
He bare it to the Cite grett,
There the kyng his fader sett
As a lord of jentiłł blood,
For he wold saue it ffro dede;
A grype flew a-bove his hede
And cryed, as he were wood.

This holy man hied hym tyte
To a Cite with touris white,
As fast as he may.
The kyng at the yate stode
And other knyghtes and lordys good
To se the squiers play.
The kyng said: 'Be Mary myld,
Yonder comyth Antony, my child,
With a gryffon gay.
Som of his byrdus take hath he,
And bryngith hem heder to me!'
Gret ferly had thaye.

The kyng there of toke good hede,
And a-geyn his sonne he yede
And said: 'Welcom ye be!'
'Fader,' he said, 'god you saue!
A knave child ffound I haue,
Loke, that it be dere to the!
Frome a greffon he was refte,
Of what lond that he is lefte,
Of gentiłł blood was he:
Thou hast none heyre, thy lond to take,
For Iesu love thy sonne hym make,
As in the stede of me!'

A knave child there he found,
There was closed in his hand
A gold ring rich and good.
He bore it to the great city,
There the king his father sat
As a lord of worthy blood,
For he would save it from death;
A griffin flew above his head
And cried, as if he were mad.

This holy man hurried himself quickly
To a city with white towers
As fast as he may.
The king stood at the gate
And other knights and good lords
To see the squires play.
The king said, "By Mary mild,
Yonder comes Anthony, my child,
With a griffin gay.
He has taken some of his young,
And brings them hither to me!"
They had great terror.

Anthony presents the child to his father and asks he take it as his son, as he himself has renounced his own nobility. The king accepts and names the child Anthony Fitzgriffin.

The king took great heed,
And went to his son
And said, "Welcome you are!"
"Father," he said, "God save you!
I have found a knave child,
Look, that it be dear to you!
From a griffin he was taken,
From what land that he is left,
Of worthy blood he was
You have no heir to take your land,
For Jesus' love make him your son,
Instead of me!"

The kyng said: 'Yf I may lyve,
Helpe and hold I shałł hym yeve
And receyve hym as my son.
Sith thou hast this lond forsake,
My riche londys I shałł hym take,
Whan he kepe them con.'
To a ffont they hym yaue,
And crystonyd this yong knave;
Fro care he is wonne.
The holy man yaue hym name,
That Iesu shild hym ffrome shame:
Antony fice greffoun.

'Fader, than haue thou this ryng,
I ffound it on this swete thing,
Kepe it, yf thou may:
It is good in euery fight,
Yf god yeve grace, that he be knyght,
Be nyght and be day.'
Let we now this children dwełł,
And speke we more of Desonełł:
Her song was welaway.
God, that died vppon the Rode,
Yff grace, that she mete with good!
Thus disparplid are thay.

This lady walkyd ałł alone
Amonge wyld bestis meny one,
Ne wanted she no Woo;
Anon the day be-gan to spryng,
And the ffoules gan to syng,
With blis on euery bowȝe . . . .

'Byrdus and bestis, aye woo ye be!
Alone ye haue lefte me,
My children ye have slone.'

The king said, "If I may live,
Help and kindness I shall give him
And receive him as my son.
Since you have forsaken this land,
My rich lands I shall give him,
When he can keep them."
They took him to a fountain,
And christened this young knave;
From grief he cried.
The holy man gave him a name,
That Jesus shield him from shame,
Anthony Fitzgriffin.

Anthony gives his father the gold ring he found in the child's hand.

"Father, then have this ring,
I found it on this sweet thing,
Keep it, if you may.
It is good in every fight,
If God gives grace, that he be a knight,
By night and by day."
Let us now leave these children,
And speak more of Desonell.
Her song was wellaway.
God, that died upon the cross,
Give grace, that she meet with good!
Thus separated they are.

Desonell, now robbed of both her children, wanders the wilderness in grief and sorrow.

This lady walked all alone
Among many wild beasts,
Never was she want for woe;
At once the day began to spring,
And the fowls sang,
With bliss on every bough. . . .

"Young birds and beasts, ever woe are you!
Alone you have left me,
My children you have slain."

As she walkid than a-lone,
She sye lordis on huntyng gone,
Nere hem she yede fułł sone.
This carfułł lady cried faste,
Than she herd this hornes blaste
By the yatis gone,
But ran in to a wildernes,
Amongist beests that wyld wes,
For drede, she shold be slone.

Tiłł it were vnder of the Day,
She went fro that wilsom way,
In to a lond playn.
The kyng of Naȝareth huntid there,
Among the hertes, that gentiłł were;
There of she was fułł ffayn . . . .

They had ferly, kyng and knyght,
Whens she come, that lady bryght,
Dwelling here a-lone.
She said to a squier, that there stode:
'Who is lord of most jentiłł blood?'
And he answerid her anon:
'This ys the lond of Naȝareth,
Se, where the kyng gethe,
Of speche he is ffułł bone;
Ałł in gold couerid is he.'
'Gramercy, sir,' said she,
And nere hym gan she gone.

Lordys anon ageyn her yode,
For she was com of gentiłł blood,
In her lond had they bene:
'God loke the, lady ffree,
What makist thou in this contre?'
'Sir,' she said, 'I wene,

As she walked then alone,
She saw lords gone hunting,
Near them she went soon.
This grieving lady cried fast,
Then she heard this horn blast
By the gates gone,
But ran into a wilderness,
Among beasts that were wild,
For dread she should be slain.

A hunting party, led by the king of Nazareth, approaches, Desonell runs to them and the king soon recognizes her (he had once sent her a prized white horse as a gift, the same horse she then presented to Torrent).

Till it were afternoon,
She went from that desolate way,
Into a plain.
The king of Nazareth hunted there,
Among the hearts that were worthy;
There she was fully glad. . . .

They had terror, king and knight,
When she came, that lady bright,
Dwelling there alone.
She said to a squire that stood there,
"Who is lord of the most worthy blood?"
And he answered her at once,
"This is the land of Nazareth,
See, where the king goes,
Of speech he is good;
He is all covered in gold."
"Many thanks, sir," she said,
And near him she went.

Lords at once went to her,
For she was of worthy blood,
In her land they had been,
"God, protect you, lady free,
What brought you to this country?"
"Sir," she said, "I know,

Seynt Katryn I shold haue sought,
Wekyd weders me heder hath brought
In to this fforest grene,
And ałł is dede, I vnderstond,
Saue my selfe, that com to lond
With wyld beestis and kene.'

'Welcom,' he said, 'Desonełł,
By a tokyn I shałł the tełł:
Onys a stede I the sent.
Lady gent, ffeyre and ffree,
To the shold I haue wedid be,
My love was on the lent.'
Knyghtis and squiers, that there were,
They horsid the lady there,
And to the Cite they went.
The quene was curtes of that lond
And toke the lady be the hond
And said: 'Welcom, my lady gent!

'Lady, thou art welcom here,
As it ałł thyn own were,
Ałł this ffeyre contree!'
'Of one poynt was my care,
And my two children crystonyd ware,
That in wood were reft ffro me.'
"Welcom art thou, Desonełł,
In my chamber for to dwełł,
Inough there in shałł ye see!'
Leve we now that lady gent,
And speke we of sir Torrent,
That was gentiłł and ffre.

The kyng of Norway is fułł woo,
That sir Torent wold wend hym ffro,
That doughty was and bold:

Saint Katherine[21] I should have sought,
Wicked weathers have brought me here
Into this green forest,
And all are dead, I understand,
Save myself, that came to land
With wild and keen beasts."

"Welcome," he said, "Desonell,
By a token I shall tell you
Once I sent you a horse.
Gentle lady, fair and free,
I should have been wedded to you,
I loved you."
Knights and squires that were there,
They horsed the lady there,
And went to the city.
The queen of that land was courteous
And took the lady by the hand
And said, "Welcome, my noble lady!"

The king of Nazareth brings Desonell home to live with him and his queen.

"Lady, you are welcome here,
As it were all your own,
All this fair country!"
"Of one point was my grief,
And my two children were christened,
In that wood were torn from me."
"You are welcome, Desonell,
To dwell in my chamber,
You shall see enough in there!"
We now leave that noble lady,
And we speak of Sir Torrent,
That was worthy and free.

After a year in Norway, Torrent is anxious to return to Portugal and Desonell.

The king of Norway is full of woe,
That Sir Torrent would go from him,
Who was brave and bold.

'Sir,' he said, 'abyde here
And wed my doughter, that is me dere!'
He said, in no wise he wold.
He shipped oute of the kynges sale
And Ryved vp in Portingale
At another hold.
Whan he herd tełł of Desonełł,
Swith on sownyng there he fełł
To the ground so cold.

The fals kyng of Portingale,
Sparid the yatis of his sale
For Torent the ffree;
He said: 'Be Mary clere,
Thou shalt no wyfe haue here,
Go sech her in the see!
With her she toke whelpis two,
To lerne to row wold she go.'
'By god, thou liest,' quod he,
'Kyng Colomand, here my hond!
And I be knyght levand,
I-quytt shałł it be!'

Torent wold no lenger byde,
But sent letters on euery side
With fforce theder to hye.
Theder com oute of Aragon
Noble knyghtes of gret renown
With grett chevalrye.
Of Pervyns and Calaber also
Were doughty knyghtes meny moo,
They come ałł to that crye.
Kyng Calomond had no knyght,
That with sir Torent wold fyght,
Of ałł that satt hym bye.

"Sir," he said, "wait here
And wed my daughter that is dear to me!"
He said, in no wise he would.
He shipped out of the king's hall
And arrived in Portugal
At another hold.
When he heard tell of Desonell,
Quickly he fell swooning
To the ground so cold.

Torrent arrives back in Portugal and learns of the king's treachery and his exiling Desonell and her children.

Enraged, Torrent calls upon the kings of Provence, Calabria, and Aragon to assist him. An army is raised to march on Portugal.

None of the knights of Portugal will fight against Torrent and his army.

The false king of Portugal,
Locked the gates of his hall
To Torrent the free;
He said, "By Mary bright,
You shall have no wife here,
Go look for her in the sea!
She took her two whelps with her,
To teach them to row she went."
"By God, you lie," he said,
"King Calamond, hear my vow!
And I am a living knight,
I shall be repaid!"

Torrent would no longer wait,
But sent letters on every side
To hasten thither with force.
Thither came out of Aragon
Noble knights of great renown
With great chivalry.
From Provence and Calabria also
Were many more brave knights
They all came to that cry.
King Calamond had no knights
That would fight with Sir Torrent,
Of all that sat by him.

There wold none the yatis deffend,
But lett sir Torent in wend
With his men euerychone.
Swith a counsełł yede they to,
To what deth they wold hym do,
For he his lady had slone.
'Lordis,' he said, 'he is a kyng,
Men may hym nether hede ne hing.'
Thus said they euerychone.
They ordenyd a shipp ałł of tree
And sett hym oute in to the see,
Among the wawes to gone.

Gret lordis of that lond
Assentid to that comnand,
That hold shold it be.
In the havyn of Portyngale,
There stode shippes of hede vale
Of Irun and of tree.
A bote of tre they brought hym be-fforn,
Fułł of holis it was born,
Howsełł and shryfte wold he.
Sir Torent said: 'Be seynt Iohn,
Seth thou gaue my lady none,
No more men shałł do the!'

The shipp-men brought sir Colomond
And sent hym fforth within a stound
As ffar as it were.
Wott ye wełł and vnderstond,
He come never ayen to lond,
Such stormes ffound he there.
Gret lordys of renown
Be-toke sir Torent the crown
To reioyse it there.
Loo, lordys of euery lond:

None there would defend the gates,
But let Sir Torrent go in
With every one of his men.
Quickly they went to council,
As to what death they would do to him,
For he had slain his lady.
"Lords," he said, "he is a king,
Men may neither behead nor hang him."
Thus everyone said.
They ordered a wooden ship
And set him out to sea,
To go among the waves.

Torrent convenes a council to debate the fate of the evil king. It is decided he will be put in a boat and cast out to sea in the same manner as Desonell. This sentence is carried out, and the king perishes at sea.

Great lords of that land
Assented to his command,
That it should be held.
In the harbor of Portugal,
There stood ships of much value
Of iron and wood.
They brought him before a boat of wood,
Full of holes it was,
Houseled and shrift he would be.
Sir Torrent said, "By Saint John,
Since you gave my lady none,
No more men shall give you!"

The sailors brought sir Calamond
And sent him forth within a time
As far as it were.
He knew well and understood,
He would never again come to land,
Such storms he found there.
Great lords of renown
Gave Sir Torrent the crown
To assume rule there.
Lo, lords of every land,

Falshode wyłł haue a foule end,
And wyłł haue euermore.

Sir Torent dwellid thare
Fourty days in moche care,
Season for to hold;
Sith he takith two knyghtes,
To kepe his lond and his rightes,
That doughty were and bold.
'Madam,' he said to the quene,
'Here than shałł ye lady bene,
To worth as ye wold.'
He purveyd hym anon,
To wend ouer the see fome,
There god was bought and sold.

And ye now wiłł liston a stound,
How he toke armes of kyng Calomond,
Listonyth, what he bare.
On asure, as ye may see,
With syluer shippes thre,
Who so had be thare.
For Desonełł is love so bryght,
His londis he takyth to a knyght,
And sith he is boun to fare.
'Portyngale, haue good day
For Sevyn yere, parmaffay,
Par aventure som dele mare!'

Sir Torent passid the Grekys flood
In to a lond both riche and good,
Fułł evyn he toke the way
To the cite of Quarełł,
As the boke of Rome doth tełł,
There a soudan lay.
There he smote and set adown

Deception will have a foul end,
And will have evermore.

Sir Torrent dwelled there
Forty days in much grief,
To hold court;
After he took two knights,
To keep his land and his rights,
That were brave and bold.
"Madame," he said to the queen,
"Here you shall be lady,
To live as you would."
He arranged at once,
To go over the sea foam,
Where God was bought and sold.

Torrent is made the new king of Portugal. He holds court for forty days before appointing two knights to administer the land and assuring the queen she is safe and free to remain as long as she wants.

And you now will listen a time,
How he took King Calamond's coat of arms,
Listen to what he bore.
On azure, as you may see,
With three silver ships,
Whoso had been there.
For Desonell is love so bright,
His lands he took to a knight,
And after he was bound to fare.
"Portugal, have good day
For seven years, by my faith,
Perhaps by some deal more!"

The grieving Torrent departs Portugal by the sea. The narrator tells us it will be more than seven years before he returns.

Sir Torrent passed the Greek sea
Into a land both rich and good,
At evening he took the way
To the city of Quarell[22],
As the book of Rome tells,
There a sultan lay.
There he smote and set down

Torrent and his army come ashore at the far end of the Grecian (Mediterranean) Sea.

He lays seige to the city of Quarell for two years before taking it.

And yaue asaute in to the town,
That wiłł the storye say.
So wełł they vetelid were,
That he lay there two yere,
Sith in the town went they.

And tho sir Torent ffound on lyve,
He comaundid with spere and knyffe
Smertely dede to be;
He said: 'We haue be here
Moche of this two yere
And onward on the thre.'
Ałł the good, that sir Torent wan,
He partid it among his man,
Syluer, gold and ffee;
And sith he is boun to ride
To a Cite there be-syde,
That was worth such thre.

There he stode and smote adown
And leyd sege to the town,
Six yere there he lay.
By the VI yere were ałł done,
With honger they were ałł slone,
That in the Cite lay.
The Soudan sent to sir Torent than,
With honger that thes people be slan,
Ałł the folke of this Cite;
'Yf ye thinke here to lye,
Ye shałł haue wyne and spycery,
I-nough is in this contre.'

Now god do his soule mede!
On the soudan he had a dede
Vppon euery good ffryday.
Iesu sent hym strengith I-nough,

And gave assault into the town,
That the story says.
They were so well provided for,
That he lay there two years,
After they went into the town.

And then Sir Torrent found life there,
He commanded with spear and knife
All to be killed;
He said, "We have been here
Much of these two years
And onward on the third."
All the goods, that Sir Torrent won,
He distributed among his men,
Silver, gold, and property;
And after he was bound to ride
To a city there beside,
That was worth as much as three.

Torrent leaves Quarell and lays siege to the next town he comes to. This siege lasts six years.

There he stood and smote down
And laid siege to the town,
Six years he lay there.
By the sixth year all were done,
By hunger they were all killed,
That lay in the city.
The sultan sent to Sir Torrent then,
That these people were killed by hunger,
All the folk of the city;
"If you think to lie here,
You shall have wine and spicery,
Enough is in this country."

Now God did reward his soul!
On the sultan he had a battle
Upon every Good Friday.
Jesus sent him strength enough,

With dynt of sword he hym slough,
There went none quyk away.
Down knelid that knyght
And thankid god with alł his myȝt:
So ought he wełł to say.
The Cite, that sir Torent was yn,
Worldely goodis he left ther yn,
To kepe it nyght and day.

Sith he buskyd hym to ride
In to a lond there be-syde,
Antioche it hight.
Sevyn yere at the Cite he lay
And had batełł euery good ffryday,
Vppon the Sarȝins bryght;
And be the VII yere were gone,
The child, that the liberd had tane,
Found hym his fiłł off ffyght . . . .

The kyng of Ierusalem herd tełł
Of this lord good and fełł,
How doughtyly he hym bare.
Vppon his knyghtes can he całł,
'Ordeyn swith among you ałł,
For no thing that ye spare!'
They buskyd hem oute of the land,
The nombre off ffyfty thousand,
Ageyn Torent ffor to ffare . . . .

The kyng of Ierusalem said thus:
'My dere son, Liobertus,
That thou be bold and wight!
Thou shalt be here and defend the lond
From that fals traytors hond
And take the ordre of a knyght.'
He yaue hym armes, or he did passe:

With a blow of his sword he slew him,
None ran away.
Down knelt that knight
And thanked God with all his might
So he well ought to say.
The city that Sir Torrent was in,
Worldly goods he left therein,
To keep it night and day.

Torrent moves on to besiege the city of Antioch. This siege lasts seven years.

By this time his son, now called Leobertus, has grown into a warrior.

After he prepared to ride
Into a land there beside,
Antioch[23] it was called.
Seven years at the city he lay
And had battle every Good Friday,
Upon the bright Saracens[24];
And by the seventh year,
The child, that the leopard had taken,
Found his fill of fighting. . . .

The king of Jerusalem heard tell
Of this lord good and strong,
How bravely he bore himself.
He called upon his knights,
"All of your prepare quickly,
Spare nothing!"
They went out of the land,
The number of fifty thousand,
To fight against Torrent. . . .

The king of Jerusalem, learning of the chaos Torrent has created, orders Leobertus and fifty thousand men to ride out and meet the invading army.

The king of Jerusalem said thus,
"My dear son, Leobertus,
That you be bold and valiant!
You shall be here and defend the land
From that false traitor's hand
And take the order of a knight."
He gave him arms before he passed

Right as he ffound was,
On gold he bare bryght
A liberd of asure bla
A child be-twene his armes twa:
Woo was her, that se it myght!

Sir Torent wold no lenger abyde,
But thederward gan he ride;
And to the feld were brought
Two knyghtes, that were there in stede;
Many a man did they to blede,
Such woundis they wrought.
There durst no man com Torent nere,
But his son, as ye may here,
Though he knew hym nought.
Ałł to nought he bet his shild,
But he toke his fader in the feld,
Though he there of eviłł thought.

Whan sir Torent was takyn than,
His men fled than, euery man,
They durst no lenger abyde.
Gret ruth it was to be hold,
How his sword he did vp-hold
To his son that tyde.
To Ierusalem he did hym lede,
His actone and his other wede,
Ałł be the kyngis side;
'Sir,' he said, 'haue no care,
Thou shalte lyve and welfare,
But lower ys thy pryde!'

Fro that sir Torent was hom brought,
Doughty men vppon hym sought,
And in preson they hym thronge.
His son above his hede lay,

Right as he found,
On gold he bore bright
A leopard of azure blue
A child between his two arms
Woe to he who might see it!

Torrent and his unknown son Leobertus meet in battle. Leobertus defeats his father and Torrent is taken back to Jerusalem and imprisoned but not executed.

Sir Torrent would no longer wait,
But rode thitherward;
And to the field were brought
Two knights that were there on horseback;
They made many a man bleed,
Such wounds they wrought.
No man dared come near Torrent,
But his son, as you may hear,
Though he knew him not.
All to nothing he beat his shield,
But he took his father in the field,
Though he thought him evil.

When Sir Torrent was taken then,
His men fled then, every man,
They dared no longer wait.
Great pity is was to behold,
How his sword he did uphold
To his son that time.
To Jerusalem he led him,
His acton[25] and his other garments,
All by the king's side;
"Sir," he said, "have no grief,
You shall live and fare well,
But lower is your pride!"

From there Sir Torrent was brought,
Brave men sought him,
And threw him in prison.
His son lay above his head,

To kepe hym both ny3t and day,
He wist wełł, that he was strong.
Thus in preson as he was,
Sore he si3ed and said alas,
He couth none other songe.
Thus in bondys they held hym thare
A twelfmonyth and som dele mare,
The knyght thought ffułł long.

In a mornyng as he lay,
To hym selfe gan he say:
'Why lye I thus alone?
God, hast thou forsakyn me?
Ałł my truste was in the,
In lond where I haue gone!
Thou gave me my3t ffor to slee
Dragons two other thre
And giauntes meny one,
And now a man in wekid lond
Hath myn armour and stede in hond:
I wold, my liffe were done!'

His son herd hym say soo
And in his hert was fułł woo,
In chamber there he lay;
'Sir,' he said, 'I haue thy wede,
There shałł no man reioyse thy stede,
Yf so be, that I may.
By oure lady seynt Mary,
Here shalt thou no lenger lye,
Nether be ny3t ne be day;
As I am Curtesse and hend,
To the kyng I shałł wend,
And ffor thy love hym pray!'

On the morow whan he Rose,

To keep him both night and day,
He knew well that he was strong.
Thus in prison as he was
Sorely he sighed and said alas,
He could sing no other song.
Thus in bonds they held him there
Twelve months and some deal more,
The knight thought full and long.

Torrent remains imprisoned for more than a year. One day Leobertus overhears him lamenting his fate to God and recounting some of his past exploits.

Leobertus takes pity on Torrent and says he will entreat the king to release him from the dungeon.

On a morning as he lay,
He said to himself,
"Why do I lie alone?
God, have you forsaken me?
All my trust was in you,
In the lands where I have gone!
You gave me might to slay
Two or three dragons
And many giants,
And now a man in a wicked land
Has my armor and horse in hand.
I know my life is done!"

His son heard him say so
And in his heart was full of woe,
In his chamber he lay;
"Sir," he said, "I have your garments
No man shall possess your horse,
If it be so, that I may.
By our lady Saint Mary,
Here you shall lie no longer,
Neither by night or by day;
As I am courteous and noble,
To the king I shall go,
For your love and pray!"

In the morning when he rose,

The prynce to the kyng gose
And knelid vppon his knee;
'Sir,' he said, 'ffor goddus sonne,
The knyght, that lieth in the dungeon,
Ye wold graunt hym me!
I hard hym say be hym alone,
Many Geauntes had he slone
And dragons II or thre.'
The kyng said: 'Be my ffay,
Be warr, he scape not away;
I vouch hym saue on the!'

The prynce in to the preson went,
Torent by the hond he hent
Oute of his bondys cold;
To the castełł he brought hym sone
And light ffettouris did hym vppon,
For brekyng oute off hold.
The kyng said: 'Be my ffaye,
And he euer scape away,
Fułł dere he shałł be sold!'
'Sir,' he said, 'parmaffay,
We wyłł hym kepe, and we may:
There of be ye bold!'

For he was curtes knyght & free,
At the mete sett was he
By the kyng at the deyse.
'Sir, thou haste i-bene
At Iustis and at tornementes kene,
Both in warr and in peas:
Sith thy dwelling shałł be here,
I pray, that thou woldist my son lere,
Hys Tymber ffor to asay.'
'Sir,' he said, 'I vnderstond,
Affter the maner off my lond

The prince went to the king
And knelt upon his knee;
"Sir," he said, "for God's son,
The knight that lies in the dungeon,
You would grant him to me!
I heard him say he alone,
He had slain many giants
And two or three dragons."
The king said, "By my faith,
Beware he not escape;
I vouchsafe him on you!"

The king reluctantly agrees to release Torrent into Leobertus' custody.

The prince went into the prison,
And took Torrent by the hand
Out of his cold bonds;
To the castle he brought him soon
And put light fetters upon him,
To keep him from breaking out.
The king said, "By my faith,
If ever he escapes,
Full dearly he shall be sold!"
"Sir," he said, "By my faith,
We will keep him as we may
Be assured of that!"

For he was a courteous knight and free,
And was sat at the meal
By the king at the dais.
"Sir, you have been
At jousts and at tournaments keen,
Both in war and in peace.
Since your dwelling shall be here,
I pray that you would teach my son,
To try his lance."
"Sir," he said, "I understand,
After the manner of my land

After hearing from Leobertus that Torrent was once a great warrior, the king asks him to teach his son the art of jousting. Torrent agrees.

I shałł, with outen delay.'

The castełł court was large with in,
They made ryngis ffor to Ren,
None but they alone.
Euery of hem to oþure Rade:
Feyrer Turnamentes than they made,
Men sye never none.
The prynce in armes was fułł preste,
Thre shaftys on his fader he breste,
In shevers they gan gone.
Sir Torent said: 'So mvt I thee,
A man of armes shałł thou be,
Stalworth of blood and bone!'

Harroldys of armes cryed on hight,
The prynce and that other knyght
No more juste shałł thay;
But lordys of other lond,
Euery one to other ffond,
And sith went theyre way.
Sixe wekys he dwellid there,
Tiłł that ałł delyuerd were,
That in the Cite lay.
Tho they held a gestonye,
With ałł maner of mynstralsye,
Tyłł the Sevynth day.

Lordis with ałł other thing
Toke leve at the kyng,
Home theyre ways to passe.
That tyme they yaue Torent the floure
And the gre with moch honowre,
As he wełł worthy was.
The kyng said: 'I shałł the yeve
Liffe and lyvelode, whiłł I lyve,

I shall without delay."

The castle court was large within,
They made rings to run,
None but they alone.
Each of them rode to the other
Fair tournaments then they made,
Men never saw such.
The prince assaulted in full arms,
Three shafts on his father he burst,
In splinters they went.
Sir Torrent said, "So I may,
A man of arms you shall be,
Stalwart of blood and bone!"

Leobertus jousts with Torrent three times, defeating him at each engagement.

Heralds of arms cried on high,
The prince and that other knight
Should no more joust;
But lords of other lands,
Every one to the other found,
And after went their way.
Six weeks they dwelled there,
Till all that were delivered,
That in the city lay.
They held a feast,
With all manner of music,
Till the seventh day.

A larger tournament is arranged that lasts for six weeks. Lords and knights from other lands come to compete. At the end of the tournament a week-long feast is held.

Torrent is honored for having won the prize at the tournament. The king, now favoring Torrent, gives him back his freedom and his armor.

Seeing many noble and beautiful ladies at the tournament, Torrent's mind drifts back to the memory of Desonell.

Lords with all other things
Took leave of their king,
To pass their way home.
That time they gave Torrent the flower
And the favor with much honor,
As he was well worthy.
The king said, "I shall give you
Life and livelihood, while I live,

Thyn armour, as it was.'
Whan he sye ffeyre ladyes wend,
He thought on her, that was so hend,
And sighed and said: 'Alas!'

The kyng of Naȝareth home went,
There that his lady lent,
In his own lede.
'Sir,' she said, 'ffor goddus pite,
What gentilman wan the gre?'
He said, 'So god me spede,
One of the ffeyrest knyghtis
That slepith on somer nyghtes
Or walkyd in wede;
He is so large of lym and lith,
Ałł the world he hath justid with,
That come to that dede.'

'Good lord,' said Desonełł,
'For goddus love ye me tełł,
What armes that he bare!'
'Damysełł, also muste I the,
Syluer and asure beryth he,
That wott I wełł thare.
His Creste is a noble lond,
A Gyaunt with an hoke in hond,
This wott I wełł he bare.
He is so stiff at euery stoure,
He is prynce and victoure,
He wynneth the gree aye where.

Of Portyngale a knyght he ys,
He wanne the town of Raynes
And the Cite of Quarelle;
At the last jurney that was sett,
The prynce, my broders son he mett,

Your armor, as it was."
When he saw fair ladies go,
He thought on her that was so noble,
And sighed and said, "Alas!"

The king of Nazareth went home,
Where his lady lived,
In his own land.
"Sir," she said, "for God's pity,
What gentleman won the prize?"
He said, "So God help me,
One of the fairest knights
That slept on summer nights
Or walked in clothes;
He is so large of limb and joint,
All the world he has jousted with,
That came to that battle."

The king of Nazareth, who was at the tournament, returns home and tells his queen and Desonell of the prowess and attractiveness of one particular knight.

"Good lord," said Desonell,
"For God's love tell me,
What arms he bore!"
"Damsel, also I tell you
He bore silver and azure,
That I know well there.
His crest is a noble land,
A giant with a hook in his hand,
This I know well he bore.
He is so stiff at every blow,
He is prince and victor,
He wins the prize everywhere.

He is a knight of Portugal,
He won the town of Raynes[26]
And the city of Quarell;
At the last journey that was set,
He met the prince, my brother's son,

And in his hond he ffeɫɫ.
The prynce of Grece leth nere
There may no juster be his pere,
For soth as I you teɫɫ:
A dede of armes I shaɫɫ do crye
And send after hym in hye.'
Blith was Desoneɫɫ.

This dede was cried ffar and nere,
The kyng of Ierusalem did it here,
In what lond that it shold be.
He said: 'Sone, anon right
Dight the and thy cryston knyght,
For sothe, theder wiɫɫ we.'
Gret lordys, that herith this crye,
Theder come richely,
Everyman in his degre.
The kyng of Grece did make hym boun,
With hym come Antony ffyȝ greffon,
With moche solempnite . . . .

'The kyng of Naȝareth sent me,
That there shold a justynge be
Of meny a cryston knyght,
And aɫɫ is ffor a lady clere,
That the justyng is cryed ffar and nere,
Of men of armes bryght.'
Gret joye it was to here teɫɫ,
How thes kynges with the knyghtis feɫɫ
Come and semled to that ffyght.

There come meny another mon,
That thought there to haue to done,
And than to wend her way.
Whan they come to the casteɫɫ gent,
A Roaɫɫ ffyght, verament,

And fell to his hand.
The prince of Greece attacked near
No jouster is his peer,
For truth I tell you
A deed of arms I shall proclaim
And send after him in haste."
Desonell was happy.

Desonell recognizes Torrent from the king's description. The king of Nazareth declares he too will arrange a tournament and invite Torrent to attend.

This deed was cried far and near,
The king of Jerusalem heard it,
In what land that it should be.
He said, "Son, at once
Prepare you and your Christian knight,
For truth, thither we will go."
Great lords that heard this cry,
Came thither richly,
Every man in his rank.
The king of Greece prepared himself,
With him came Anthony Fitzgriffin,
With much ceremony. . . .

Word of the new tournament reaches the king of Greece who declares he will attend and bring his son, Anthony Fitzgriffin.

"The king of Nazareth sent me,
That there should be a jousting
Of many a Christian knight,
And all is for a fair lady,
That the jousting is cried far and near,
For men of bright arms."
Great joy it was to hear told,
How these kings with the brave knights
Came and assembled for that fight.

There came many other men,
That thought there to have done,
And then to go their way.
When they came to the noble castle,
A royal fight, truly,

There was, the sothe to say.
Trompes resyn on the wałł,
Lordys assembled in the hałł,
And sith to souper yede thay.
They were recevid with rialte,
Euery man in his degre,
And to her logyng went her way.

The lordys Rosyn ałł be-dene
On the morow, as I wene,
And went masse ffor to here.
And ffurthermore with-oute lent
They wesh and to mete went,
For to the ffeld they wold there.
After mete anon right
They axid hors and armes bryght,
To hors-bak went thay in ffere.
Knyghtis and lordys reuelid ałł,
And ladyes lay ouer the castełł wałł,
That semely to se were.

Than eueryman toke spere in hond,
And euerych to other ffond,
Smert boffettes there they yeld.
The prynce of Ierusalem and his brother,
Eueriche of hem Ran to other
Smertely in the feld . . . .
Thoug Antony ffygryffon yonger were,
His brother Leobertus he can down bere;
Sir Torent stode and be-held.

'Be my trouth,' said Torent thanne,
'As I am a cryston man
I-quytt shałł it be.'
Torent be-strode a stede strong
And hent a tymber gret and long,

There was, to say the truth.
Trumpets rose on the wall,
Lords assembled in the hall,
And after they went to supper.
They were received with royalty,
Every man in his degree,
And to their lodgings went their way.

The lords rose immediately
In the morning, as I know,
And went to hear mass.
And furthermore without delay
They washed and went to eat,
For to the field they would go,
At once after the meal.
They asked for horses and bright arms,
And went in company on horseback.
Knights and lords all in revelry,
And ladies lay over the castle wall,
That were seemly to see.

At the tournament, the brothers Anthony Fitzgriffen and Leobertus meet in the joust. Though he is the younger, Anthony emerges victorious.

Torrent, seeing Leobertus defeated, rides out to defend his honor.

Then every man took spear in hand,
And each to the other found,
Smart blows there they paid.
The prince of Jerusalem and his brother,
Each ran to the other
Smartly in the field. . . .
Though Anthony Fitzgriffin was younger,
He bore down his brother Leobertus;
Sir Torrent stood and beheld.

"By my truth," Torrent said then,
"As I am a Christian man
Acquitted shall it be."
Torrent mounted a strong steed
And seized a lance great and long,

And to hym rode he.

Torrent to hym rode so sore,
That he to the ground hym bare,
And let hym lye in the bent.
There was no man hyȝe ne lowe,
That myght make Torent to bowe
Ne his bak to bend.
They justyd and turneyd there,
And eueryman ffound his pere,
There was caught no dethis dent.
Of ałł the Justis, that there ware,
Torent the floure a way bare
And his sonnys, verament.

And on the morow, whan it was day,
Amonge ałł the lordys gay,
That worthy were, par de,
Desonełł wold no lenger lend,
But to sir Torent gan she wend
And knelid on her kne.
She said: 'Welcom, my lord sir Torent!'
'And so be ye, my lady gent!'
In sownyng than fełł she.
Vp they coueryd that lady hend,
And to mete did they wend
With joye and solempnite.

Dame Desonełł be-sought the kyng,
That she myght, with oute lesyng,
Sytt with Torent alone.
'Yes, lady, be hevyn kyng,
There shałł be no lettyng;
Worthy is he, be seynt Iohn!'
Tho they washid and went to mete,
And rially they were sett

And rode to him.

Torrent rode to him so fiercely,
That he bore him to the ground,
And let him lie in the grass.
There was no man high nor low,
That might make Torrent bow
Nor bend his back.
They jousted and turned there,
And every man found his equal,
There were no death blows caught.
Of all the jousts, that there were,
Torrent bore away the flower
And his sons, truly.

Torrent bests Anthony Fitzgriffin and every other knight who challenges him to win the prize.

And in the morning when it was day,
Among all the happy lords,
That were worthy, by God,
Desonell would no longer rest,
But to Sir Torrent she went
And knelt on her knee.
She said, "Welcome my lord Sir Torrent!"
"And so it be you, my noble lady!"
Then she fell in a swoon.
They recovered that lady,
And went to a meal
With joy and solemnity.

The next morning Torrent and Desonell are finally reunited.

Dame Desonell besought the king,
That she might, without lying,
Sit with Torrent alone.
"Yes, lady, by heaven's king,
There shall be no delaying;
He is worthy, by Saint John!"
Then they washed and went to dine,
And royally they were set

And seruid worthely, echone.
Euery lord in the hałł,
As his state wold be-ffałł,
Were couplid with ladyes schone.

But of ałł ladyes, that were there sene,
So ffeire myght there none bene
As was dame Desonełł . . . .
Thes two kyngis, that doughty ys,
To the Cite come, i-wys,
With moche meyne emell.

To the castełł they toke the way,
There the kyng of Naȝareth lay,
With hym to speke on higȝ.
At none the quene ete in the hałł,
Amongist the ladyes ouer ałł,
That couth moche curtesye.
Desonełł wold not lett,
By sir Torent she her sett,
There of they had envye . . . .

Whan eyther of hem other be-held,
Off care no thyng they ffeld,
Bothe her hertes were blithe.
Gret lordys told she sone,
What poyntes he had for her done,
They be-gan to be blithe;
And how her fader in the see did her do,
With her she had men childre two;
They waried hym fełł sithe.
'Sir kyng, in this wildernes,
My two children fro me revid wes,
I may no lenger hem hide.
The knyght yaue me rynges two,
Euerich of hem had one of thoo,

And served nobly each one,
Every lord in the hall,
As his state would befall,
Were coupled with beautiful ladies.

But of all ladies that were seen there,
None might there be so fair
As was dame Desonell. . . .
These two kings, that were brave,
Came to the city, I know,
With many men together.

To the castle they took the way,
There the king of Nazareth lay,
To speak with him on high.
At noon the queen ate in the hall,
Amongst all the ladies,
That knew much courtesy.
Desonell would not delay,
By Sir Torrent she sat,
Thereof they had envy. . . .

Torrent and Desonell retire with the king of Nazareth to dine. At the meal Desonell recounts her past misfortunes and the loss of her two children.

When either of them beheld the other,
They felt no grief,
Both their hearts were joyful.
Great lords told her soon,
What deeds he had done for her,
They began to be happy;
And how her father cast her in the sea,
With her she had two boy children;
They cursed him bitterly afterward.
"Sir king, in this wilderness,
My two children were torn from me,
I may no longer hold them.
The knight gave me to two rings,
Each of them had one,

Better saw I never none.
A Gryffon bare the one away,
A liberd the other, parmaffay,
Down by a Roche of stone.'
Than said the kyng of Ierusalem:
'I ffound one by a water streme,
He levith with blood & bone.'
The kyng of Grece said: 'My brother,
Antony my son brought me anoþure.'
She saith: 'Soth, be seynt Iohn?'

The kyng said: 'Sith it is so,
Kys ye youre fader bo,
And axe hym his blessyng!'
Down they knelid on her knee:
'Thy blessing, ffader, for charite!'
'Welcom, children ying!'
Thus in armes he hem hent,
A blither man than sir Torent
Was there none levyng;
It was no wonder, thouȝe it so were;
He had his wiffe and his children there,
His joye be-gan to spryng.

Of ałł the justis, that were thare,
A way the gre his sonnys bare,
That doughty were in dede.
Torent knelid vppon his knee
And said: 'God yeld you, lordys ffree,
Thes children that ye haue ffed:
Euer we wiłł be at youre wiłł,
What jurney ye wiłł put vs tyłł,
So Iesu be oure spede,
With that the kyng thre
In to my lond wiłł wend with me,
For to wreke oure stede.'

I never saw better.
A griffin bore the one away,
A leopard the other, by my faith,
Down by a cliff of stone."
Then said the king of Jerusalem,
"I found one by a stream,
He lives with blood and bone."
The king of Greece said, "My brother,
Anthony my son brought me another."
She said, "Truth, by Saint John?"

The king of Jerusalem tells Desonell he found one of her children and that the other was rescued by his brother, the king of Greece.

The king said, "Truth it is so,
Kiss your father both,
And ask him his blessing!"
Down they knelt on their knee
"Your blessing, father, for charity!"
"Welcome, young children!"
Thus in his arms he took them,
A happier man than Sir Torrent
There was none alive;
It was no wonder, though it were so
He had his wife and his children there,
His joy began to grow.

Torrent and Desonell are reunited with their lost children.

Of all the jousts that there were,
His sons bore away the prize,
That were brave in battle.
Torrent knelt upon his knee
And said, "God reward you, lords free,
These children that you have fed.
Ever will we be at your will,
What journey you will put us to,
So Jesus be our fortune,
With that the three kings
Into my land will go with me,
To avenge our home."

Torrent tells the kings of Greece and Jerusalem that he and Portugal will always be their allies for having rescued and raised his sons.

They graunted that there was,
Gret lordys more and lesse,
Bothe knyght and squiere;
And with Desonełł went
Al the ladyes, that were gent,
That of valew were.
Shippis had they stiff and strong,
Maistis gret and sayles long,
Hend, as ye may here,
And markyd in to Portingale,
Whan they had pullid vp her sayłł,
With a wynd so clere.

The riche quene of that lond
In her castełł toure gan stond
And be-held in-to the see.
'Sone,' she said to a knyght,
'Yonder of shippis I haue a sight,
For sothe, a grett meyne.'
The quene said: 'Verament,
I se the armes of sir Torent,
I wott wełł, it is he.'
He answerid and said tho:
'Madam, I wiłł, that it be so,
God gefe grace, that it so be!'

A blither lady myȝt none be,
She went ageyn hym to the see
With armed knyghtes kene.
Torent she toke by the hond:
'Lordys of vncouth lond,
Welcom muste ye bene!'
Whan she sye Desonełł,
Swith in sownyng she fełł
To the ground so grene.
Torent gan her vp ta:

That was granted,
Great lords more and less,
Both knight and squire;
And with Desonell went
All the ladies that were noble,
That were of value.
They had ships stiff and strong,
Masts great and sails long,
Taken, as you may here,
And sailed into Portugal,
When they had pulled up their sails,
With a wind so clear.

Torrent and his family, the kings of Greece and Jerusalem, and a party of knights take to ships and sail for Portugal.

The rich queen of that land
Stood in her castle tower
And looked out into the sea.
"Young man," she said to a knight,
"I have sight of yonder ships,
For truth, a great many."
The queen said, "Truly,
I see the arms of Sir Torrent,
I know well, it is he."
He answered and said then,
"Madame, I know, that it be so,
God give grace that it be so!"

The queen of Portugal greets Torrent upon his return and is overcome at the return of her daughter Desonell and her children.

There might be no happier lady,
She went again to him to the sea
With armed knights strong.
Torrent she took by the hand,
"Lords of heathen land,
Must have welcomed you!"
When she saw Desonell,
Quickly she fell in a swoon
To the green ground.
Torrent took her up,

'Here bene her children twa,
On lyve thou shalt hem seene!'

In the Castełł of Portyngale
A-Rose trumpes of hede vale,
To mete they went on hye.
He sent letters ffar and nere;
The lordys, that of valew were,
They come to that gestonye.
The Emperoure of Rome,
To that gestonye he come,
A noble knyght on hyȝe.
Whan ałł thes lordys com were,
A justyng did he crye.

So it ffełł vppon a day,
The kyng of Ierusalem gan say:
'Sir, thy sonne I ffound
Lying in a libertes mouth,
And no good he ne couth,
Dede he was nere hond:
Wold thou, that he dwellid with me,
Tiłł that I dede be,
And sith reioyse my lond?' . . . .

Be fore lordys of gret renown,
Torent gaue hym his son . . . .
The kyng of Grece said: 'Sir knyght,
I yeff thy son ałł my right
To the Grekys flood:
Wouch thou saue, he dwełł with me?'
'Yea, Lord, so mut I thee,
God yeld you ałł this good!'
For sir Torent was stiff in stoure,
They chose hym ffor Emperoure,
Beste of bone and blood.

"Here are her two children,
Alive you shall see them!"

Games and feasts are arranged on the happy occasion of the family's return.

The kings of Greece and Jerusalem ask Torrent to permit his sons to remain with them, to be their heirs and inherit their respective kingdoms. Torrent agrees.

Torrent is then made the new emperor of Portugal and the other lands he was awarded for his past deeds.

In the castle of Portugal
Trumpets of great value arose,
To dine they went quickly.
They sent letters far and near;
The lords that were of value,
They came to that celebration.
The emperor of Rome,
He came to that celebration,
A noble knight on high.
When all these lords had come,
A jousting he cried.

So it fell upon a day,
The king of Jerusalem said,
"Sir, your son I found
Lying in a leopard's mouth,
And he was helpless,
Death was near at hand.
Would you permit that he dwell with me,
Till I die,
And after possess my land?" . . . .

Before lords of great renown,
Torrent gave him his son. . . .
The king of Greece said, "Sir knight,
I give your son all my right
To the Greek sea.
Would you permit he dwell with me?"
"Yea, lord, so I must,
God reward you all this good!"
For Sir Torrent was upright in battle,
They chose him for emperor,
Best of bone and blood.

Gret lordys, that there were,
Fourty days dwellith there,
And sith they yode her way;
He yaue his sonnys, as ye may here,
Two swerdys, that were hym dere,
Ech of hem one had they.
Sith he did make vp-tyed
Chirchus and abbeys wyde,
For hym and his to praye.
In Rome this Romans berith the crown
Of ałł kerpyng of Renown:
He leyth in a feire abbey.

Now Iesu Cryst, that ałł hath wrought,
As he on the Rode vs bought,
He geve hvs his blessing,
And as he died for you and me,
He graunt vs in blis to be,
Lesse and mare, both old and ying!
Amen.

Explicit Torent of Portyngale.

Torrent presents his two prized swords, Adolake and Mounpolyardnus, to his sons before they depart.

After ruling for an indeterminate period, Torrent dies and is buried in an abbey.

The narrator states that this tale is chief among all the known romances of renown.

Great lords, that were there,
Forty day dwelled there,
And after they went their way;
He gave his sons, as you may hear,
Two swords, that were dear to him,
Each of them had one
After he built
Churches and abbeys wide,
For him and his to pray.
In Rome this romance bears the crown
Of all talking of renown.
He lays in a fair abbey.

Now Jesus Christ, that has made all,
As he on the cross bought us,
He gave his blessing,
And as he died for you and me,
He grants us to be in bliss,
Less and more, both old and young!
Amen.

End Torrent of Portugal.

Notes

1. Southeastern geographic region of France.
2. Possibly a reference to the French city of Pérrone, though geographically this city is neither in the south of France nor located at the seaside.
3. Legendary blacksmith and armorer from Norse and Germanic mythology.
4. City located in present day Israel. In biblical texts, once the home of Jesus.
5. Some legends arising in the Middle Ages suggest that Mary Magdalene fled the Holy Land after the crucifixion of Jesus and eventually settled in the Provence region of France where she converted the people there to Christianity. Some of these legends also purport that she died and was buried there.
6. Cave in Provence near the present town of Saint-Maximin-la-Sainte-Baume. Legend holds Mary Magdalene lived here for nearly thirty years.
7. Saint James the Greater. One of the twelve apostles of Jesus. Likely beheaded by King Herrod Agrippa I before AD 44.
8. Medieval kingdom located in northern Spain. Currently one of Spain's seventeen autonomous communities.
9. Region of southern Italy occupying the toe of the Italian peninsula's "boot".
10. There have been numerous Saint Adrian's throughout history. This reference is most likely Saint Adrian of Nicomedia martyred in AD 306.
11. Given its geographic distance from Calabria, it is unlikely this is a reference to the region occupied by modern day Hungary. No definitive source can be found identifying where this specific city might have been located.
12. Most likely Saint Augustine of Hippo (AD 354–430).
13. Sources differ on whether this refers to the Spanish towns of Cardona or Cordova.
14. No reference can be found identifying the origin of any Saint Griffin.
15. Possibly the town of Carrión de los Condes located in present day autonomous Spanish community of Castile and León
16. Nicholas of Myra (AD 270–343). Also known as Nicholas of Bari, he was known for presenting unexpected gifts and is the foundational figure for the modern-day Saint Nick, Santa Claus.
17. Not a reference to the present-day country of Brazil. Middle Age legends held of a mythical island in the ocean west of Ireland. Maps as late as 1480 still displayed its possible location.

18. George of Lydda (AD 303). Early Christian martyr most notable for the legend of his defeating a dragon in combat.
19. Likely a crude pun made in reference to sexual intercourse where the woman staddles a prone man.
20. There have been numerous individuals bearing the moniker Saint Anthony, several of whom were described as hermits. These include Anthony the Great (AD 251-356), Anthony of Antioch (AD 266–302), and Anthony of Padua (1195–1231). Given the proximity to the town of the same name, it stands to reason this figure is modeled on Anthony of Antioch.
21. Catherine of Alexandria (4th c. AD). Virgin martyr used in the medieval period as an example of proper feminine behavior.
22. No historical reference for the existence of this city can be located.
23. Greek city founded in 300 BC in southern Turkey. Later served as a regional capital in both the Roman and Byzantine empires. The city of Antakya stands in its place today.
24. Medieval European term denoting the nomadic Arab and Muslim peoples of the present-day Middle East. As Muslims, the Saracens were often depicted as the enemies of Christianity.
25. Also known as a gambeson. A padded wool or linen coat worn as armor or in conjunction with a suit of plate or mail armor.
26. No definitive reference can be located that reliably identifies this city.

www.ingramcontent.com/pod-product-compliance
Lightning Source LLC
LaVergne TN
LVHW090520110826
845146LV00003B/926

* 9 7 9 8 9 9 3 4 3 2 6 1 8 *